Critical acclaim
for Joyce Carol Oates's

SOLSTICE

"Oates is superb, convincing . . . her latest novel should remind us of the important place Joyce Carol Oates occupies in American letters as a novelist of the first rank."

—*Newsday*

". . . a craftsman . . . a storyteller . . ."

—*Newsweek*

"Enormously readable . . . Joyce Carol Oates manages to exhilarate . . . with the sheer vitality of her prose."

—Joyce Maynard, *Mademoiselle*

"She has wrought a minor miracle. There's such immediacy to this story, it reads as though it had been ripped out of her."

—*New Woman*

Berkley Books by Joyce Carol Oates

MYSTERIES OF WINTERTHURN
SOLSTICE

Solstice

JOYCE CAROL OATES

BERKLEY BOOKS, NEW YORK

This Berkley book contains the complete
text of the original hardcover edition.
It has been completely reset in a typeface
designed for easy reading and was printed
from new film.

SOLSTICE

A Berkley Book/published by arrangement with
E. P. Dutton, Inc.

PRINTING HISTORY
E. P. Dutton edition published 1985
Berkley edition/October 1986

ISBN: 0-425-09204-6

This book is for S., the only begetter—

After great pain, a formal feeling comes—
The Nerves sit ceremonious, like Tombs—
The stiff Heart questions was it He, that bore,
And Yesterday, or Centuries before?

The Feet, mechanical, go round—
Of Ground, or Air, or Ought—
A Wooden way
Regardless grown,
A Quartz contentment, like a stone—

This is the Hour of Lead—
Remembered, if outlived,
As Freezing persons, recollect the Snow—
First—Chill—then Stupor—then the letting go—

EMILY DICKINSON, 1862

CONTENTS

SOLSTICE

PART I

The Scar

1

IT WAS ON a mild, fragrant evening in late September, several weeks after she had moved to Glenkill, Pennsylvania, to begin teaching at the Glenkill Academy for Boys, that Monica Jensen was introduced to Sheila Trask at a crowded reception in the headmaster's residence. And the meeting was so awkward, her own response so lacking in brilliance or distinction, Monica could never have predicted that Sheila Trask would remember her or even that they would see each other again.

From the very first, when she visited Glenkill to be interviewed for her position the previous spring (as one, she uneasily gathered, of a half-dozen candidates of "superior qualifications"), Monica had been aware that the artist Sheila Trask lived most of the year in the Glenkill area. She owned one of the old Bucks County estates, an early-nineteenth-century house called Edgemont, which her husband, the sculptor Morton Flaxman, had left her. So far as Monica knew Sheila Trask had only a minor national reputation but she seemed to enjoy a certain local celebrity—though it might have been notoriety.

(A number of artists evidently lived in Bucks County at the present time. None was so famous as Andrew Wyeth, who lived in Chadds Ford, some distance to the south, but their names were nonetheless mentioned occasionally, as if by accident: conversational nuggets that might be examined, and contemplated, or allowed to be dropped, depending upon one's inclination. The gentlemen who had taken Monica to lunch at an inn on the Delaware River, and who had interviewed her for two hours, so discreetly and casually she might have mistaken the experience for a mere social encounter, brought up Sheila Trask's name; and the name of her late husband Flaxman. Fortunately for Monica she knew Flaxman's work—knew enough to say a few intelligent and appreciative things about it, though she wasn't unstintingly enthusiastic: the heavy white masses, the unbroken lines and featureless curves, the mere *semblance* of living, primitive forms, had always vaguely troubled her, weighed upon her vision, as she sat with a cooling cup of tea—one cup after another, in fact—in the sculpture garden of the Museum of Modern Art, trying to find a way out of the cul-de-sac of her life. But at least she could envision something when Flaxman's name was mentioned; so far as Sheila Trask was concerned—she could envision nothing at all. And as she looked from Mr. Greene, the headmaster of the school, to Mr. Farley, who chaired the English Department, Monica could not determine whether this readily admitted ignorance was in her favor or against her. "Miss Trask's paintings are experimental, I suppose it might be said," Mr. Greene said, smiling, "—powerful—and abstract—and difficult to describe." Monica murmured, not quite apologetically, that she knew very little about contemporary art, either American or European—she was afraid she found most of it flat, inhuman, sterile, and oddly unimaginative. "Yes. Exactly," Mr. Greene said.)

Then, in the early summer, when Monica was taken by a real estate agent to look at various rentals in the area, she was again informed, casually, that Sheila Trask would be practically a neighbor of hers if she rented the house—a five-bedroom farmhouse—she wanted most. Of course, the real estate agent added, it wasn't likely she would ever meet Sheila Trask since the woman was always traveling. And she spent a great deal of time in New York. She was reclusive, perhaps a bit eccentric, unpredictable, hard to please—so the local merchants said—not universally liked. Monica had hesitated to seem inquisitive—she wanted, here in Glenkill, to establish another sort of reputation altogether—but Betty Connor seemed so guileless, so genuinely friendly, she couldn't resist asking in what ways Sheila Trask was eccentric. "Various ways," Mrs. Connor said, retreating at once, "I don't know her personally, of course. . . . Maybe you'll meet her yourself." Did she go out of her way to be disagreeable? Monica asked. "Well," said Mrs. Connor, "the first thing you'd, say about her isn't that she's disagreeable, in fact she's usually charming, very charming, she appeals to a certain kind of man—and woman too, I suppose. But maybe you'll meet her yourself. Then you can form your own judgment."

By the time of the Greenes' party, months later, Monica had quite forgotten about Sheila Trask. In the strain and exhaustion and frequent euphoria of her first weeks of teaching Monica had forgotten a great deal: she had become, rushing from place to place, trying cheerfully to memorize a hundred or more new names, a kind of amnesiac—her earlier life, her earlier preoccupations, had been wonderfully blotted out. Many years ago she had been a golden girl of sorts—she had even looked rather golden—and now it seemed to her that another shadowless epoch of her life might be imminent. *If she proceeded with caution. If she behaved very, very prudently.*

"I don't remind myself of myself at all," Monica murmured aloud, amused. "I seem to be so happy."

She had surprised everyone who knew her, ex-husband in particular, by accepting an invitation to teach at a private boys' school in rural Pennsylvania. Surely she might have done better? Surely she might have waited until something more congenial turned up? But in this phase of her life Monica was done with waiting for the reward, or the fate, she deserved; she was eager to make do with comparatively little. She was eager simply to forget.

So when, at the Greenes' spirited party, she had happened to see a tall, dark-haired, rather slovenly dressed woman enter the room, Monica had thought only that she was odd—arresting—a "character" in some not fully tangible way. She was a woman five or six years older than Monica, in her midthirties perhaps, and attractive enough, even—almost—beautiful, with derisive black eyes and heavy unplucked black brows and a wide, unsmiling, quizzical mouth. Her figure was almost painfully angular; her shoulders were sloping, her posture slouched. Unlike the Greenes' other guests she had not taken the occasion seriously enough to dress for it—she wore a shapeless black skirt that fell unevenly to midcalf, and a cheap much-laundered cotton shirt, and what appeared to be a man's tweed jacket, unbuttoned, and drooping from her thin shoulders. An odd bird of prey, Monica thought, maneuvering where she could observe the woman more easily.

She wore flat-heeled shoes of no discernible style, mud- or paint-splattered; and her legs, pale and luminous, and somewhat sinewy, seemed to be bare. Her stride was brash, perhaps horsey—she was certainly a horsewoman or a sportswoman of some kind—she leaned forward to shake hands, jerking her elbow downward in an unusual manner, not feminine (whatever, Monica thought, *feminine* precisely means) but not masculine either: rather in the style of a self-conscious and slightly sulky adolescent. There was something edgy about her, something mirthless yet jocular, an air of the improvisational and the uncoordinated: she had pinned a white camellia to her untidy hair in a romantic (or a mock-romantic) gesture, but the flower now hung wilted and forgotten as if about to fall. While Harry and Ruth Greene turned their animated attention upon her she frankly surveyed the room, rocking on her heels, her hands inelegantly thrust into her pockets. Alone in this chattering smiling crowd she was unsmiling and appeared to be replying to the Greenes in monosyllables. Monica supposed her a guest of no little significance, judging from the attention paid her by the headmaster and his wife—and now the chaplain and *his* wife—and several other persons of importance. Perhaps she was the wife of a trustee or a trustee herself, Monica thought, though she was rather young for the role. No doubt she lived on one of the splendid country estates in the area, no doubt she rode thoroughbred horses; there was something arrogant about her stance, the slight, almost imperceptible bend of her knees. . . . She was clearly well-to-do and assured, the kind of woman Monica usually avoided.

Yet there was something familiar about her too—the black gypsyish eyes, the fleshy mouth, the restless manner. The way her gaze sifted through the crowd, idle, predatory, seemingly aimless. Monica wondered for a brief excited moment whether they might have met before. It would probably have been in New York City if anywhere. Though she and her husband had had surprisingly few friends in the two years they had lived in the city they seemed to have been acquainted with a great many persons, a variegated promiscuous number, strangers with "familiar" faces, friendly enough at parties, in fact wonderfully friendly at parties, though otherwise anonymous. . . . The black-haired woman struck Monica as quintessentially New York despite her horsey posture: but when her prowling gaze touched upon Monica there was no sign of recognition or interest.

"That woman over there, the one with the amazing eyebrows," one of Monica's male colleagues said in a low voice, "—the one who looks as if she's wandered in and is about to wander out again—that's Sheila Trask the painter: does she look anything like her photographs?"

"I've never seen a photograph of her," Monica said.

A few minutes later Mrs. Greene led Monica over to the woman, and introduced them in a hearty voice, as if "Miss Trask" might actually be interested in "Miss Jensen," one of the promising new instructors on the Glenkill faculty. She clearly offended Sheila Trask by suggesting that the two women were practically neighbors: Monica had just moved into a farmhouse on the Olcottsville Road, and Sheila lived at Edgemont, on the Poor Farm Road, approximately two miles to the north. "I'm afraid I really don't have any neighbors, Edgemont is so isolated," Sheila Trask murmured. Her voice was both apologetic and incensed. But she shook hands readily with Monica in her stilted mock-formal way.

Her fingers were thin, cold, surprisingly strong. She wore no rings and her nails had been bluntly filed; even so they were ridged lightly with dirt or paint. She gave off a mingled scent—tobacco, turpentine, wool in need of dry cleaning, the faint sweet odor of the wilted camellia. Close up, Monica saw that she was even thinner than she had appeared at a distance, but wiry, sinewy. She was probably in her early forties. Her skin looked exotic, soiled—it had a queer olivish tint that suggested malnourishment. Her black, moist, slightly protuberant eyes were her most beautiful feature: thickly lashed, deep-set and shadowed, and suspicious. And the unplucked black brows nearly met in a querulous inverted V on the bridge of her nose.

Out of politeness she asked Monica one or two questions about the house she had rented, and Monica's answers were brief, shy, not very inspired. Ruth Greene, smiling and maternal, led another junior instructor forward to be introduced; there were more murmured exchanges; smiles, handshakes; a few awkward though well-intentioned remarks about Sheila Trask's work. (These the frowning woman accepted in absolute silence—as if she had heard nothing.) But the young man blundered onward, cleared his throat and declared that he was a "staunch admirer" of Morton Flaxman's work as well. "He'd be honored to know that," Sheila Trask said with a flash of malicious gaiety, "if he were alive."

When Monica left the reception a half-hour later she saw that Sheila Trask had already gone; she must not have stayed more than twenty minutes. Odd, Monica thought, that she had troubled to come at all—she so clearly felt conspicuous, talked-about, ill at ease. And superior to the Glenkill people.

On the flagstone walk outside the residence Monica noticed a limp and torn white flower—a camellia—and had the impulse, for an inexplicable moment, to pick it up.

"You'll get married again," friends told her, not knowing how their words stung, and Monica said with as much dignity as she could manage, "Yes—there are different kinds of marriage."

It had not been for the salvation of her soul—she didn't any longer believe in either "soul" or "salvation"—but for simple survival that Monica had come to teach at the Glenkill Academy (prestigious, costly, conservative, *Founded 1847*, as the plaque boasted, by *The Society of Friends);* and to put her past behind her. Survival was a clear, frank, unpretentious matter, a primitive need which she hoped to cultivate, with hard work and idealism, into something approaching a life.

She, who had always been young, was now a few months from her thirtieth birthday. She was scarred—yes literally and not *merely* figuratively—by her recent inglorious past: in fact she often found herself stroking her barely visible three-inch wound, her prize, her bitter solace. "Look what you've done to me, look what you've *done,*" she had cried in triumph, her first instinct being to accuse, to gloat, to deliver a wound herself which she hoped might be lethal. But the blood had been hers.

It wasn't true precisely that Monica Jensen had been a golden girl, though she liked the expression—she was reminded by it of Shakespeare's grim lyric. ("Golden lads and girls all must,/ As chimney-sweepers, come to dust.") A wonderful false democratizing here, a suggestion that all human beings are equal in Infinity, hence why envy, spite, sorrow, pain, unhappiness _now_—? Small consolation for the chimney sweepers who died young, not only turning to dust but dwelling in it, in life; but immense consolation to the golden lads and girls who need not feel guilt for their selfish privilege. Monica saw herself unsentimentally as a woman, a former _girl,_ who had had power—derived from where, she couldn't have guessed—to convince others, for a while, of her goldenness, her specialness. The emotional logic of loving _her._

She had been married at the age of twenty-one, and divorced at the age of twenty-nine. There were eight years to account for, more or less. (She had begun living with her fiancé in what had been imagined as a defiant gesture, seven or eight months before they were married. But neither his family nor hers had chosen to respond to the defiance.) She was beginning to forget a great deal. She had already forgotten a great deal. The dailiness of their lives —at which they were not very skilled—was rapidly retreating, leaving behind stark and isolated events, mere incidents, things that had happened and were therefore meant to illuminate their participants: the marriage, the ill-timed pregnancy, the abortion, the mourning, the silence . . . and the rest. Monica told herself sternly that if her experience had been special it would be wicked of her to forget it: but it hadn't been special, it belonged to too many people of her generation.

The marriage and its breakup were bracketed by two opposing—yet not dissimilar—ceremonies. They too had

become impersonal events. Time, which had always un-
folded in an uncomplicated motion, vaguely allied with
"improvement" or "progress," had cruelly pleated: so that
Monica had no sooner become accustomed to thinking of
herself as a married woman than she was no longer married. She had been plunged into a tunnel and before her
eyes could become accustomed to the dark she had been
forced out of it again, dazed, shaken, considerably older.
After eight years she was "herself" again—*Jensen* and not
Bell—whatever that meant. Instead of sharing a three-
room apartment off Sixth Avenue with a man said to be her
husband she was living, alone, in a five-bedroom shingle-
board farmhouse a mile beyond Glenkill, Pennsylvania. It
was a region she hadn't known existed before the previous
spring: the serenity and calendar-art beauty of its rolling
farmland and woodlands and unpaved roads and lanes
seemed to harbor, in its very perfection, a subtle undefined
threat to her sense of reality. Or to her sense of what she
deserved. ("Do you think you can walk away from all
this?" her husband had said, his voice trembling with
hatred; and Monica had had no reply that she dared utter
aloud.)

But the divorce had gone through just the same. And
she was free, as he was. (By way of mutual acquaintance
she had learned that he was on the West Coast, working for
a cultural foundation of sorts in San Francisco. They had
told her the name—the foundation was evidently sup-
ported by one of the oil conglomerates—but Monica
wasn't certain she remembered it correctly.) In Glenkill she
was alone and undefined and in a curious battered way
virginal again. How does it feel at the age of twenty-nine
to be the object of no one's desire, she queried herself—
no one's love, no one's particular interest? How does it feel
to be able to sleep through most of the night? To be able to
work efficiently for twelve or more hours a day? Since

moving into her farmhouse on the day before Labor Day
Monica had experienced several voluptuous attacks of
sheer anxiety—that she did not deserve her good fortune
and would be punished. Then again she thought, gloating:
"But I won't be punished!—I did walk away without being
struck in the back."

How does it feel, Monica boasted to her mirror reflection,
to be so exhausted you wouldn't be capable of crying if
there were any reason to cry—?

Her chairman had assigned her six days of classes,
including a third-form composition class that met on
Saturday mornings at eight o'clock: put her on several
committees: named her as faculty adviser to one of the
student organizations. By magic she had become "Miss
Jensen" to her students, "Monica" to her new colleagues,
whose names she prided herself upon memorizing in the
first two weeks. She didn't at all mind that she had, in all,
more than one hundred students (which meant, among
other things, more than one hundred weekly themes to correct): she was in fact grateful for the opportunity to demonstrate just how hard she could work without even
good-humored complaint. She liked being exhausted, it
had become a kind of drug to her, like walking for hours
—for hours and hours—in Manhattan, up from Eleventh
Street to Central Park in a drunken zigzag pattern, not
minding the airlessness and midsummer heat and the ex-
haust of those ubiquitous buses. She loved being so drained
of energy, so wrung dry, that, before midnight, she could
only set the alarm for six-thirty the following morning and
fall into bed. (Where her dreams were hallucinatory, ca-
reening and vertiginous, rapid flashes of bizarre images
played against the raw insides of her eyelids.)

She was prevented, consequently, from dwelling upon
the past, which was after all *past*. She was prevented from

lapsing into self-pity and self-recrimination and self-loath-
ing of the kind she so abhorred in women acquaintances of
hers whose marriages had "also" ended disastrously. How
did I fail, these stunned women asked themselves, and
what did I do wrong, how could I have avoided . . . ? *I, I,
I . . .*

After her first week of teaching Monica had been so
stupefied with exhaustion she hadn't been able to complete
her grocery shopping at the Olcottsville A & P—she left
the part-filled cart in one of the aisles and made her way,
blinking and light-headed, out to her car.

When she had free hours, on the weekends in particular,
she worked at the house, scouring away layers of grime,
washing windows, sanding, polishing, preparing to strip
wallpaper, deliberating over which rooms to paint and
which simply to close off. And should she borrow money
to make improvements and buy furniture, or should she
restrict herself to what she could afford, month by month
—? She had not felt so powerful a sense of ownership and
domesticity since the earliest months of her marriage when
the setting—the exact, the *absolute* setting—for hers and
her husband's passion had come to matter more than the
passion itself.

The chimneys, Mrs. Connor had warned her, probably
leaked; the cellar would *probably* flood if there was a great
deal of rain. There were loose-fitting windows and shingles
nearly rotted through and the condition of the two remain-
ing barns was frankly dangerous—she shouldn't go prowling and poking around in them, in the hayloft in particular:
the owner of the property had seen to it that a clause had
been added to the lease exempting him from responsibility
along these lines. Nonetheless Monica indulged in day-
dreams of buying the farm one day. The three-acre property
had once included several hundred acres of meadow- and
farmland and woods, and she fantasized buying them all

back. On three sides she had views of open meadows and farmland, on the fourth side a view of her own weather-worn barns, no other human habitation was in sight; the Olcottsville Road, narrow and poorly paved, had very little traffic. . . . She recalled Sheila Trask's annoyance at the suggestion that they were neighbors and felt now the logic of it. The woman hadn't meant to be insulting—she had simply stated a self-evident truth.

Sometimes, when she was vacuuming or running water she imagined she heard the telephone ringing, but when she stopped to listen she heard nothing—only silence. She received very few telephone calls and made few; nor did she receive much mail. All of which soothed her if it did not entirely please her. The house exuded indefinable odors of age and dust, and sometimes, particularly at night, it seemed to echo with unknown lives and histories: but Monica told herself she was safe here, out in the country, as she had rarely been safe in Manhattan. She shared the house with no one. There was never the possibility of an-other person slamming open any door she had closed, or calling her name . . . Though once or twice she imagined she heard her name spoken aloud: Monica: faintly, lightly: *Monica—!* But not in the cadence of her former husband's voice. In the cadence of no voice she knew.

She had plans, she calibrated certain strategies, she was a professional woman and no fool, despite her fading golden looks and her soft-spoken manner. She would sink herself for the next ten months in the very pettiness of her work: preparing lessons, correcting student papers (in such fastidious detail everyone would marvel at her idealism), teaching to the best of her abilities, attending meetings, being congenial—but not too eagerly congenial—to her colleagues. To reward herself she would turn her attentions to the house. Scouring sinks and tubs, caulking, varnish-ing, painting, buying curtains, gay-striped blinds, cushions, pillows. . . . Though her husband had contemptuously given all the furniture to her Monica had been able to furnish only a few rooms of this large house, so there were months ahead, absorbing, self-indulgent months, of browsing through secondhand furniture shops in the county, searching for bargains. She would buy old lamps, old clocks, umbrella stands, antique books . . . she would prop herself up in bed and read novels by authors whose names were long forgotten, romances of the Brandywine and the Delaware valleys, books whose covers were falling off and whose pages were yellowed. . . . A second marriage, Monica thought. Of sorts.

Time had pleated so queerly, swallowing up eight years of her life. But now it would expand. Now clocks would tick with less urgency. She would never again think of injuring herself, blaming herself, loathing herself. She would never again lie in rumpled sheets smelling of her own sweat and misery, thinking, How have I failed, what have I done wrong, what are the flaws in my character. . . .

"But why think of the past? Where *is* the past?" Monica said aloud, suddenly angry. She reveled in the sound of her own voice when it was angry. When no one else was a witness.

2

ONE AFTERNOON IN early October Monica was leaning in the doorway at the rear of the house when she happened to notice a horse and rider appear at the edge of a woods some distance away. A man or a woman?—she squinted but couldn't be sure. It was a warm day, the sunshine blazed. The air was loud with insects. Monica waited for another rider to appear behind the first—she'd seen as many as five or six riders on that lane—and when no one else came along, and the rider turned in her direction, she felt a clutch of fear.

It wasn't fear, precisely. It must have been simple alertness, apprehension. She didn't want anyone intruding on her privacy.

But she didn't withdraw into the house. She stared, squinting into the sun, raptly absorbed as the rider drew closer—now cantering, now trotting—in a display of high spirits. Monica knew very little of horses but she thought the horse—an enormous chestnut with a high-held head and white markings—was a beautiful creature: and the rider, leaning slightly forward in the saddle, appeared to be beautifully in control. "It's her," Monica thought.

She could not think of the woman's name for a few confused moments, then she remembered: Sheila Trask. But she wouldn't have dared say it aloud, she wouldn't have known what form was appropriate. Not "Sheila," surely. But "Miss Trask" was an absurdity.

Sheila Trask greeted Monica's smile with an apology, rapidly and not altogether audibly murmured, for dropping in uninvited. But she happened to be riding in the area. She was curious too about what Monica had done with the old

Dorr place—a couple named Dorr had owned it some years ago, acquaintances of Sheila's and her husband's— she remembered the house as charming in ways and problematic in others. And she could use a glass of ice water. . . .

"Of course, come in, please come in," Monica said. She added, blushing, a little rattled: "I was watching you ride and you ride so well, I was hoping you'd turn into someone I know, and— But of course I don't know anything, really, about horses—about horseback riding—"

Something affronted and hesitant in Monica's voice, some subtle flicker of reluctance in her expression, must have struck Sheila Trask: for a long strained moment she remained sitting stiffly in the saddle, her hands locked at the base of the horse's neck, regarding Monica with frank searching eyes. She was a very attractive woman in a harsh, rather slapdash way. Her black eyes glinted with something derisive and covert, a childlike offer of complicity, mutual recognition. At the same time she clearly shrank from misjudging her welcome and being rejected. She spoke so quickly and in so low a voice Monica could barely hear. ". . . if I'm interrupting your work, or your plans . . . if you have another visitor. . . ."

"No, not at all," Monica said.

"But I *am* uninvited. . . ."

"Please have a drink," Monica said, "ice water or whatever you'd like—I mean, or whatever I have—I think there's grapefruit juice and soda pop—some wine—of course," Monica said quickly, feeling her cheeks burn, "—it isn't first-rate wine, I mean, it probably isn't anything you would want—"

"Are you sure?" Sheila Trask asked, staring at her.

But Monica was sure, Monica protested that she was sure, feeling ridiculous in her unbecoming old clothes, standing in a doorway waiting for a visitor: she hardly knew what she was saying or what she really felt. "I've been working since early this morning . . . I'd like to stop for a while . . . I mean I'd like very much to . . ."

"Well—I don't want to intrude," Sheila said slowly. She dismounted, fussed with the horse, wrapped the reins around a fence post, looping and knotting them swiftly as she spoke. ". . . I know what it's like, people dropping by. You assume you're safe in the country and then unexpected visitors turn up because they're lonely and you're put in an awkward position. . . . You do remember me, don't you? We met at the Greenes'? *Sheila—?*"

Monica protested that she certainly knew who she was but hadn't known how to address her.

"'Sheila' is fine," she said, laughing.

She was perspiring freely and slightly breathless. Her brown jodhpurs were soiled, her cotton pullover shirt was stained at the armpits, her riding boots were well-seasoned with dirt and manure. Her hair was remarkably thick, yet lusterless, frizzy, exploding out about her head as if with an excess of nervous energy. In the brilliant October sunshine she looked both malnourished and oddly flushed, exuberant.

"And I remember your name—Monica? Yes. But your last name was muddled, I didn't quite hear—"

Monica told her the name and they shook hands and at the strong dry touch of Sheila's hand she felt an unaccountable sensation of panic, lasting hardly more than an instant, a fluttering in the chest, an unpleasant constriction of the throat. Afterward Monica was to conclude that she had felt vulnerable at this moment because she'd come close to telling Sheila her married name, which had been Bell. And that would have been a hateful blunder.

Of course Monica had planned on opening her house to visitors—colleagues from school primarily, and students, and any friends who cared to make the trip—but she

wouldn't have done so, she wouldn't have felt psychologi-
cally prepared, for several weeks. It hurt her pride to be
forced to see the skimpiness of her life through another's
eyes, to risk evoking pity, or displaced sympathy. Now
Sheila Trask of all persons was striding into the house, into
the kitchen, as if she had been there many times and knew
her way around. A brash, pushy, disagreeable person,
Monica thought, her cheeks burning more intensely than
before, even as her voice rattled away like that of any
good-natured friend or neighbor, assuring Sheila that she
certainly *was* welcome, she was in fact her first visitor, and
perhaps she could offer Monica advice, much-needed
advice.... Monica had never rented a house in the country
before; she had never rented a house at all. And this one
was so special, so large.... Clearly it would present so
many problems....

To which Sheila Trask replied merely, as no one else in
her situation would have done: "Yes. You're right."

She was still panting slightly and in the close quarters of
the kitchen she smelled frankly of perspiration. And of the
horse as well—Monica supposed it must be the horse—
something gamey, rank, leathery—not altogether unpleasant but certainly distracting.

And—yes—Monica's keen gaze dropped to her boots
—she would certainly trail dirt about. And take no notice
of what she did.

They settled on iced tea for both of them—fortunately
Monica had made up a pitcher that morning. Sheila said
she was dying of thirst. The sun was warmer than she'd
expected. With no more self-consciousness than a child she
tore off several paper towels from a roll lying on Monica's
kitchen table and wiped her wet face.

Monica showed her through the uncarpeted dining
room, into the living room, speaking of the house and its
problems, supplying the pretext for a conversation as

Sheila, saying very little, looked about inquisitively. She was slightly taller than Monica and moved in an erratic fashion—now quickly, now in a languid slantwise step. Her mouth was wide, fleshy, mobile, but her smiles were rather more nervous tics than anything else, and often when it seemed she was about to reply to one of Monica's remarks she said nothing at all. An odd person, Monica thought, but, oddly, charming: even rather attractive: the quick darting eyes in particular. And the strong cheekbones. The long straight nose.

She told Monica that she and her husband had known the couple who had owned the house some years ago; in fact, they themselves had owned the property for a while, for a reason never altogether clear to her: tax purposes? But now it belonged to someone who lived in Philadelphia and who couldn't be bothered with it—a pity, since it was so beautiful, so private. And lonely. "You've just moved out from Manhattan, have you?—someone was telling me," Sheila said. "That horrible woman, the chaplain's wife. She was talking about you."

Monica laughed, surprised. She felt an immediate sisterly pleasure at Sheila's intimate tone, but really didn't know how to respond to it—the chaplain's wife, Jill Starkie, had been extremely kind to her since her arrival in Glenkill, and seemed quite clearly a warm, generous, well-intentioned person, like her husband, James; it was hardly proper for Monica to pass judgment on her. Certainly Mrs. Starkie was a rather florid personality, given to hand-clutching and embraces, and an enthusiasm that could be most fatiguing, but Monica was grateful for her warm regard. So she replied carefully to Sheila's remark, supplying only a modicum of information: yes, she had just moved from New York, she had taught part-time for years but never in a preparatory school, it was all quite new to her, the immersion in the school's life, the intensity . . .

wonderfully challenging. . . . The change in her life had been badly needed. . . .

Sheila strode about the living room, a lithe, trim figure in her stained jodhpurs and white cotton shirt, curious as a child, examining the rattan furniture, the mismatched tables and chairs, the fine-grained Scandinavian bookshelves, the pale green carpet Monica had bought at a remnant outlet in Edgarsville for thirty-five dollars. Though Sheila said nothing Monica's heart lifted with the hope that Sheila approved of the things, the jumble of textures and colors and styles, one or two costly items amidst the "bargains." She didn't in any case sneer at them.

Sheila drained her iced tea and set the glass down on a pile of student papers. She said, idly: "A change badly needed? Some sort of trouble with a man? You have that dazed precarious look, it's one of the visible symptoms, but charming in its way, as if you were carrying your life in a pyramid of eggs. . . ." She made a gesture, turning her hands palm upward, extending the fingers. ". . . Though the image isn't very likely. But you know what I mean. Someone happened to mention that you were recently divorced and that Glenkill wasn't a very hospitable place for single women. All in the same breath. But it *is* a hospitable place for a single woman, don't be deceived. Don't let them coerce you into feeling lonely."

Monica was taken aback by this rush of words and had no idea how to reply. Sheila said, more thoughtfully: "Don't let them coerce you into anything. Harry Greene is famous—I should say infamous—for working his junior faculty like dogs."

Monica managed to say, with a fair degree of spirit and conviction, that she hadn't found Glenkill at all lonely so far and she didn't consider the work load at the school extraordinary, she liked in fact to work, she liked to feel herself strained to the limits, she was coming to believe she

might be a born teacher. . . . And the Greenes and the Starkies and a number of others had been extremely helpful so
far. . . . Her voice rattled on. She was slightly shaken by the
woman's frank, intimate, yet oddly negligent tone, the way
she glanced at Monica, half-smiling, her sloe eyes narrowed and her heavy black brows nearly meeting at the
bridge of her nose. So this was Sheila Trask? The woman
about whom everyone spoke in ambiguous terms, puzzled,
vaguely disapproving, clearly in awe?—yet certainly a
stranger to most of them.

In the midst of Monica's defense of her situation Sheila
drifted away and went to examine her bookshelves, squatting to look at the lower shelves. She did no more than
grunt a vague reply to Monica: rude gesture in anyone else,
but probably quite incidental, even innocent, in Sheila
Trask. Monica's words trailed off into silence and she
thought, her cheeks burning as painfully as ever, that it was
appropriate, it *was* the correct response, she had only been
chatting away nervously and inconsequentially, she could
not have said whether she meant these things or not, only
that she *ought* to mean them. . . . Sheila ignored her for
some minutes, pulling paperback books out and examining
them with sudden interest. Her black hair had frizzed badly
in the humid air but gave her a kind of hoydenish charm.
Her thin cotton shirt was damp with perspiration and
strained tight against her back, showing every bony knob
of vertebrae; wisps of curly hair glistened beneath her
arms. She might have been twenty years younger than her
age, not a woman of distinction, surely not the widow of
Morton Flaxman.

Monica, staring at her, could not decide whether she
disliked Sheila Trask intensely and wished her gone, or
whether she felt the tug of a powerful attraction.

Sheila began to muse aloud, saying she envied Monica
her books, these particular books (orange-spined Penguin

copies of the Brontës, Dickens, George Eliot, Trollope), they were so dog-eared and worn, so marked with under-linings and annotations, it was obvious their reader had not simply read the novels but had lived through them. Of what value was a novel, Sheila asked, if one couldn't live through it?—if it were only a matter of words skill-fully arranged? She was herself so caught up in her work, not trapped, exactly, but caught up, immersed, for years she had been obsessed with "figuring certain problems out visually," she had all but abandoned reading; she had certainly abandoned these leisurely, massive, world-embracing Victorian novels. And she envied the form it-self. She envied a profession that concerned itself with books, pages, *print*. The printed line, after all, is so or-derly and chaste, so chronologically determined—that is, the reader is obliged to read line by line, page by page, in sequence; very unlike the visual image, which assaults the eye out of nowhere, in a manner of speaking, with no prep-aration, and no power over the viewer to demand from him more than a moment's casual contemplation. How it sick-ened her, how it drove her wild, to observe patrons of art museums as they drifted and dallied along, their eyes brushing against masterpieces, skimming a row of paint-ings by Vermeer or Monet or Mondrian, it scarcely mattered, the human eye is so unintelligent, so unin-formed. . . . And of course being present when her own paintings were on display was torture. . . .

Monica ventured timidly to agree. She could imagine the strain, she doubted that she herself would ever have had the courage to risk such exposure. Even if, she added, she had faith in her talent. That is—if she *had* talent.

Sheila chose to ignore this haphazard remark. She was musing, thinking aloud: ". . . Morton used to say there was something wholly sane about a book . . . because there is something finite about it. The book, no matter its length, encompasses a complete world. It *is* a world. But it displaces virtually no space in this world. Consider its size, its weight . . . set beside a massive piece of sculpture or a large canvas. God, how I envy that. The compression, the modesty . . . the sanity. . . ."

She rose rather unsteadily to her feet and fumbled in her jodhpurs pocket for something—a package of cigarettes, most likely—which wasn't there. Her fingers came away vexed, stymied. She said suddenly that she had better be going, a houseguest was expected at Edgemont that evening, she hadn't prepared anything, in any case she had intruded upon Monica long enough. . . . Monica naturally protested that she had not intruded at all. She had only arrived, really; wouldn't she care to sit down for five minutes and rest? . . . wouldn't she like another glass of iced tea?

Sheila appeared gratified by the invitation but declined it. She had only ridden over, she said, on a whim, a kind of glimmering of . . . but she didn't know what: was Monica interested in horses? Somehow she had had the erroneous idea that . . . hadn't someone told her . . .

Monica said hesitantly that she did have an interest in horses, in learning to ride. But she'd never had lessons. And she was probably rather uncoordinated and out of condition. . . .

Sheila smiled one of her brusque ticlike smiles and said, not altogether tactfully, that Monica was past the age for riding lessons, for any kind of serious commitment to riding. "You should be a young adolescent," she said. "Twelve, thirteen years old. That's when it begins. That's when the urge starts. You find that you want to grip a horse between your legs and it's a passion, a sudden passion, chaste, exquisite, almost religious. All the horses are stallions—even the mares. You could ride and ride all day and at night you dream about riding, about the horse, *your* horse. A few years later it starts to fade, this passion. It gradually disappears in most girls. With some of us, with me, for instance, it becomes a lifelong preoccupation, but you're the kind of girl, I suspect, in which it would have faded long ago."

Monica, faintly shocked, laughed at her guest's outspoken manner—this peculiar combination of rudeness and solicitude. "I see. I see," she said. "I didn't know."

Sheila was pacing again about the room, her hands on her hips, her stride loping, boyish. She examined the lighting fixtures which, she said, the Dorrs had had installed: but neither of them had much taste. She examined the ornate plaster moldings, the marble mantel (cracked in two places) above the fireplace, and the aluminum-framed print from the Museum of Modern Art above that, a brightly colored, airy, shadowless Bonnard for which, suddenly, Monica felt some subtle shame. It was a poor choice, surely? But what would Sheila Trask have suggested?

Monica watched her, fascinated, amused. She had tracked dirt onto the carpet without noticing, she'd left the row of paperback books disturbed. Her insolence was remarkable; but one couldn't take offense—for there she was, simply and defiantly herself. She displaced a great deal of air. She was assuredly not modest. Soiled jodhpurs, unshaven underarms, horsey scent, the sloe eyes quick-darting and shamelessly inquisitive.... In the slanted light from one of the high windows, however, rose-tinted by damask curtains Monica had hung only the day before, she looked quite beautiful: even gravely and uncannily beautiful.

But it was only for an instant. Immediately she turned, continued her pacing, her disjointed remarks.

(Indeed, as Monica was to remember afterward, Sheila's conversation became increasingly directionless and antic at this point.)

She expressed the hope, rather vaguely and hurriedly, that Monica would visit her at Edgemont soon. For dinner perhaps.

She made the observation that Monica must be an object of unusual interest at the Glenkill school: being one of no more than a half-dozen women, and certainly the youngest and most attractive, teaching at an all-boys school.

She apologized for having been so dogmatic about riding lessons: of course women Monica's age, and older, did take lessons: and no doubt enjoyed them thoroughly. So if Monica was sincerely interested and wanted to know the names of some reliable riding instructors in the area . . .

They might even go out riding together sometime, she said. (But in a vague trailing voice that carried with it very little conviction.)

She shifted back to the subject of the Dorrs, the house's previous owners. She and her husband had known them slightly, hadn't entirely approved of them—they were summer people primarily, connected with the Olcottsville Playhouse, histrionic, hard drinkers, dilettantes, rather gaudy and glamorous, famous for telling cruel but uproarious stories about people behind their backs. But there was nothing significant to tell Monica about them. They were cruel and careless and shallow—all surfaces. The only "event" connected with their tenancy of the house—if Sheila remembered correctly—was a shooting accident. Mrs. Dorr had snatched up a revolver and fired several shots at a bird—a starling, most likely—that had blundered down through the chimney and was flying panicked through the house, but of course the shots went wild, she nicked her husband in the ear, broke a windowpane or two, of *course* the idiotic woman was drunk, both the Dorrs were drunk, as it turned out. "It's the kind of malicious tale they liked to invent about other people," Sheila said. She was edging toward the door; clearly it was time to leave.

She lifted her eyes—bright, suddenly smiling—to Monica's face. "At least you can't be haunted by them," she said. "They weren't evil or profound. And as far as I know they're still living—in Europe, I think."

As they walked out Monica expressed some humorous disappointment that the house had been owned by such people. She had had a romantic idea that . . . she didn't entirely know what. . . . The house, the old barns, the countryside . . .

Sheila pointed out that the Dorrs were very recent, scarcely worth mentioning, in fact: the house had probably been built just after the Civil War and had been lived in by a great many people. If it was "haunted" Monica hoped to be . . .

Monica protested that she didn't hope to be "haunted": she wasn't that sure. Only inspired, perhaps. Drawn a bit out of herself and her own time. Her own history.

Sheila observed that Monica didn't have the appearance of a superstitious person in any case. Blond, healthy, forthright. A daylight personality.

"'Daylight' and not 'nocturnal,' you mean?" Monica asked. She tried to smile to disguise the queer hurt and annoyance she felt; the corners of her mouth ached. "But is it that easy to judge other people?—by appearances?"

Sheila's lips stretched from her teeth in a semblance of a grin. "You forget who you're speaking to," she said.

"What?" Monica said, half-frightened. "I don't understand."

"You're speaking to an artist—a painter," Sheila said. She flexed her long supple fingers mockingly. "I put my faith only in appearances. In paint. On canvas. In two dimensions."

As soon as the woman left Monica poured herself a glass of red wine, hurriedly, and carried it upstairs, to the room at the rear of the house she was using as a bedroom. Her footsteps echoed with a surprising urgency beneath the high ceilings; the floorboards creaked. Monica knew that Sheila Trask expected her to watch her ride away, trotting briskly along the edge of the neighboring cornfield, back to the lane by the woods. She knew, whether or not she did watch, Sheila would assume she had.

She was nearly faint with exhaustion. The visit had lasted less than half an hour—she herself had said very little—but she was as drained of energy as if she had been teaching all day. How odd, how alarming, was she actually going to faint . . . ? She leaned weakly against the window-sill and pressed her warm forehead against the pane, watching the horse and rider, noting with envy Sheila Trask's posture, her absolute naturalness and grace, every motion of hers perfectly coordinated with her mount's. Ease, confidence, bravado, a kind of self-mockery in the very effortlessness of her performance. . . . "She knows she is being watched," Monica thought. "It has been her life."

She watched the chestnut gelding trot out of sight. It was a remarkable thing, really, if you considered it—a human being, a woman, astride an animal of that size: the animal's spirit brought under control, its powerful muscles subordinate to a human will. One must either master his horse or be mastered by him, Monica had once been told. Neither prospect greatly appealed to her.

She drained the glass of wine; her head was throbbing. Sheila Trask was gone and now the house seemed inordinately quiet. Monica felt so exhausted she had an impulse to lie down fully clothed on her bed and surrender to sleep, to a groggy afternoon nap. . . . Instead she went into her bathroom and turned on the cold water faucet and splashed cold water fiercely onto her face. She slapped her warm cheeks: she was angry with herself for being so fatigued.

Her image in the mirror was subtly blurred and discolored by the old glass. Unnaturally bright eyes of no discernible color, flushed cheeks, a forehead raised in small anxious creases. The three-inch scar that ran along her lower jaw, which she had once believed would alter her life, had faded over the months and was now nearly invisible. She often found herself stroking it unconsciously, however, though she hated the sensation. She wondered if she had been touching it during Sheila Trask's visit. And whether the woman had noticed. She stared so hard at everything.

They would probably not meet again, Monica thought.

Early the following week Monica happened to encounter Sheila in Glenkill as one woman was leaving the post office and the other entering. Sheila, wearing an old belted sweater and paint-splattered jeans, was studying something in her hand, frowning at a slip of paper, and when she glanced up at Monica her black stare was piercing and ungiving: then she smiled: and the two women found themselves greeting each other with the happy avidity of friends—whose mutual feeling, whose mutual *affection,* had evidently grown in their absence. "Monica, what are you doing here?" Sheila asked, as if they had met in a remote spot, and Monica, laughing, said: "What are *you* doing here?"

It was a heady, disorienting sensation, a very odd development—a friendship that had taken root and grown in secret, without their conscious knowledge or guidance. Monica had never experienced anything quite so remarkable before. She warmly accepted Sheila's invitation to come to dinner the following night—if she could find Edgemont. "You'll find it," Sheila said. She added: "I'll come by at seven and pick you up."

3

So it began.

In the weeks that followed the two women saw each other frequently, except when Sheila was away (in New York City? in Philadelphia? elsewhere?)—rarely less than once a week, often as many as three or four times. They spoke very little on the telephone since Sheila hated the telephone—she felt crippled, she said, she felt aphasiac, if she couldn't gesture with her hands as she spoke—but they had lengthy and immensely absorbing conversations in one or the other of their houses, or in Sheila's studio. There was so much to say, so much that suddenly demanded to be said. . . . Monica realized she had been desperately lonely without knowing it. And she was a little dazed, and certainly flattered, by Sheila Trask's interest in her.

"Really—!" Sheila would say, staring at Monica. "How odd. How fascinating. But could you explain—?"

And Monica saw that—perhaps—she *was* fascinating.

Their conversations were invariably intense, even strained, lasting well past midnight even on weeknights, and leaving Monica as depleted of energy and as nervously invigorated as if she had been exercising in the fresh air. Her senses alert, her attitude somewhat combative. . . . Waking the next morning in her bed, sleep-dazed, groggy, her energy not fully restored, Monica could remember vividly Sheila Trask's flashing dark eyes and animated features, her laughter, her somewhat strident voice—she could remember the way things looked in Sheila's wildly cluttered studio, or the delicate blue and white designs of the French ceramic tiles in Sheila's kitchen, which Sheila had inlaid herself: she could remember these things clearly but she often had difficulty recalling what she and Sheila had discussed for so many hours. Sheila asked questions and Monica answered and sometimes Sheila questioned her more closely and sometimes Sheila spoke passionately.... The very intensity of their conversations and their occasional disagreements seemed to consume their actual words, as if such dreamlike agitation had to be surrendered by day.

Monica was to remember, however, objecting one evening to a pattern that had developed in their relationship: while she spoke freely enough, confiding to Sheila a number of things she had never told another person, Sheila invariably stiffened whenever Monica asked her about herself—about her marriage, her childhood, her family. Sheila would rub her face vigorously and mutter that Monica couldn't possibly want to know such things—*she* hadn't lived a very interesting life—*she* had put everything of significance into her painting—and there was nothing left over. Also, Sheila really didn't remember very much of her life. "I'm a wheel moving along the ground," she said, making a playful flamboyant gesture, "—I'm the present tense—where I touch the ground—only where I touch the ground—only in motion." When she was slightly drunk she spoke in a singsong voice that was both childlike and belligerent.

Monica said sharply: "And the rest of us aren't, in your opinion?"

"The rest of you aren't required to be," Sheila said.

Monica felt at this instant the woman's sense of her natural superiority, as casually revealed as if she had tossed a coin on the table between them. But she had no reply, no declaration of her own—she sat mute, staring.

Sheila wondered if it didn't strike Monica, from time to time, as—well, slightly inappropriate: her position as a young and very attractive woman instructor at a boys' school? Of course the Glenkill students were highly motivated and competitive—they were said to be unusually well-behaved for boys of that age—but they *were* adolescents, after all, they could hardly control the drift of their thoughts, the contents of their dreams and fantasies. And, certainly, Monica must figure predominantly in their fantasies.

So Sheila observed, eyeing her shrewdly.

Monica blushed with irritation. But she didn't inquire what sort of fantasies Sheila meant.

The subject might have been dropped, but Sheila said, after a moment: "Though perhaps you don't mind. It's a species of romance, after all."

From acquaintances in Glenkill Monica learned that the Flaxmans, as they were locally known, were an "unusual" couple; had had a "somewhat experimental" marriage. They traveled a good deal, not only to Europe but to distant, exotic parts of the world—Afghanistan, New Guinea, Patagonia. Sometimes they disappeared for months and no one knew where they had gone. Sometimes one of them would disappear and the other—why, the other would behave as if nothing at all were wrong. Or be consoled—openly and unashamedly—by an alliance of his or her own. There were houseguests of an "eccentric" sort who stayed for months, there were reports of wild parties, drinking, drug taking, fights, *very* bizarre behavior—hadn't a cast-off mistress of Morton Flaxman's once showed up at Edgemont with a gun?—hadn't a Jamaican lover of Sheila Trask's once gone berserk with a poker? ("Of course," Monica was cautioned, "this is all second- or thirdhand gossip and can't be entirely credited.")

Morton Flaxman had been twenty-three years older than Sheila Trask at the time of their wedding: forty-two to her nineteen, and already a sculptor of national prominence. He had stood six feet four inches tall and had weighed perhaps two hundred forty pounds. The words invariably applied to him in print—"Gargantuan," "Rabelaisian," "Falstaffian"—quite appealed to Monica, who was nevertheless grateful not to have to meet the man. (Flaxman was said to have been, like many male sculptors, an "avid connoisseur" of women; but he hadn't been nearly so promiscuous as his legends would have it. In fact in some quarters he was considered a "remarkably loyal" husband . . . he had stayed married, after all, for seventeen years.)

Studying a photograph of Flaxman taken a year or two before his death, Monica was struck by his massive yet courtly—kindly—appearance. He was a visibly aging man, but not yet old, bearded, near-bald, contemplative, paternal. His shoulders were broad and muscular, his wrists thick, but the position of the part-clasped hands was graceful, with an Oriental delicacy and hesitation. Monica saw with a thrill of envy why a young woman like Sheila Trask might have fallen in love with him—at one time in her life, at least.

According to Monica's Glenkill informants Flaxman had died of a cerebral hemorrhage in a distant city—Tokyo, or perhaps Calcutta—in what were said to be "ambiguous circumstances." (In a brothel of some kind? Monica couldn't help but wonder. Or had he been with a traveling companion Sheila knew nothing of?) He had died intestate but since he hadn't any surviving children from his two previous marriages, and no close relatives, Sheila Trask must have inherited his entire estate—property in Bucks County and elsewhere, art holdings, investments. It was locally assumed that Sheila Trask was a millionairess several times over, despite the way in which she dressed (considered willfully slovenly by some, merely casual and "Bohemian" by others), and the condition of the battered

Honda station wagon she drove, and her rumored frugality
at Edgemont. (It was whispered that Sheila had become
criminally negligent since her husband's death—she was
letting the old house go simply because she couldn't be
bothered with it.) The twenty-room stone-and-stucco
house, impressive rather than beautiful, but decidedly impressive, had been built in 1830 by a Glenkill squire, and
there were numerous parties, including the Bucks County
Historical Society, keen on buying it: but Sheila Trask
showed no inclination to sell. She was stubborn, she was
indifferent, she was coy, she was simply waiting for a very
high bid?...though perhaps she was sentimentally at-
tached to the property and couldn't bring herself to part
with it at any cost. She was said to have insulted a Glenkill
woman when asked about her "plans" for the future and for
the house: "'Plans'? What do you mean by 'plans'? Why
should I have any 'plans' about anything? Why should *you*
be concerned—?" And all in response to an utterly innocent question.

Monica knew that Sheila's words were literal—*merely*
literal. She had no plans for the future or for Edgemont,
she had no plans for herself, because her mind didn't oper-
ate that way. Her mind operated in far different and far
more fascinating ways.

She may have been a millionairess technically speaking,
but she worried a great deal about money in the way that
persons with a primitive sense of economics and Fate
worry about money: helplessly, despairingly, in frenzied
bouts unrelated to actions or decisions. She was superstitious as well: she told Monica in all seriousness that a
"good" year for her art always signaled a "bad" year for
her life, and vice versa; and if her paintings sold well in a
specific year it simply meant that, the following year, Internal Revenue would demand a costly audit. ("They hated

my husband and they hate me," she told Monica, white-lipped with passion. "They want to destroy artists because they hate art—they want to drain us all dry.") Morton had died six years before—Sheila had been thirty-six at the time—and his financial affairs were only now being sorted out. It was all hell, it was sheer chaos, she kept from running berserk only by tossing things into drawers, not opening envelopes with certain return addresses, handing everything over to her accountants in Philadelphia two or three times a year. (But she couldn't trust her accountants either. She had inherited them from Morton who hadn't trusted them but had resigned himself to their tricks.) So far as Edgemont was concerned—the house was one hundred fifty years old, many of the outbuildings were a century old, everything was in continual need of repair, not only actual repair but the contemplation of repairs to come, and she didn't have the time to think about such petty things, she didn't have the energy, the spirit, nor could she trust local contractors—they were notorious for gouging widows. Morton had quarreled with virtually every contractor in the area anyway, so if she wanted work done—if she even wanted estimates made—she would have to find someone a considerable distance away. But she couldn't trust strangers either. . . . (Monica said, laughingly, "But who *can* you trust, Sheila?" and Sheila said, unsmiling, seeing no joke in the question, "I really don't know.")

So far as the art world was concerned—Sheila lapsed into a furious monologue one night at Monica's house, drunk on Moët Chandon she had brought for them to have with dinner, saying that her husband had been cheated during his lifetime as a consequence of his indifference—his Olympian contempt—for dealers, publicity, critics, collectors: and now that he was dead, and his sculpture was worth a great deal, things were in such a muddle that she couldn't cope with them and get on with her own work.

"He was being cheated and now I'm being cheated and why should I make myself sick with worry?" she said. "But I do worry—I can't help it—then suddenly I find myself not giving a damn—weeks go by and I don't even think about it—it's as if I hadn't ever known Morton Flaxman, let alone slept with him for seventeen years." She paused, rubbing a fist into her rather bruised-looking eye. "Ultimately—I suppose I *don't* give a damn. I could walk away from Edgemont tomorrow and never give it a second thought as long as I could keep on working somewhere else. I don't feel like the widow of a famous man. I don't *feel* like anyone's widow—I'm simply too selfish."

Monica volunteered to help Sheila with her bookkeeping, or with checking for needed repairs on the house, whatever—even typing up forms and labels for her artwork—and Sheila stared at her as if she were mad. "With your teaching schedule, with all you have to do, where could you possibly get the time?—you're being ridiculous," she said, "you're begging to be exploited. Morton would have said yes, yes at once, yes sweetheart, do climb aboard, but I'll just say *No thank you.*" Then she added, as if she couldn't resist detaching herself, distancing herself, from Monica's solicitude: "Also—I value my privacy."

Another day, however, she would come up with the sudden idea that she should lend Monica money so that Monica could make repairs and improvements on *her* house; perhaps she should even lend Monica enough money to make a down payment toward buying the house . . . ? "Or I might buy it myself," she said vaguely, excitedly, "and you could rent it from me for a hundred dollars a month. Or would that be too much?"

She acquired a credit card and insisted upon using it when she and Monica were together. (Occasionally the two women met for lunch at the pretentious Olcottsville Inn, where Sheila was deferred to as "Mrs. Flaxman" and treated with a solemnity she found amusing; at other times, dressed in jeans and sweaters, they drove out to a country tavern on Highway 29. Early on in their friendship they fell into the custom of meeting in Glenkill's sole Chinese restaurant on Wednesday evenings, since Wednesday was Monica's most arduous day at school: she began teaching at seven-forty-five in the morning and wasn't finished with various extracurricular duties until nearly six in the evening.) Impulsively, Sheila bought Monica presents—a beautiful Shetland sweater, a pair of hand-tooled leather boots, a four-foot-high orange tree in a wooden tub. ("It would look so beautiful in that alcove in your dining room.") Monica was embarrassed to accept these gifts, more embarrassed to refuse them, and it seemed virtually impossible to make Sheila understand that her charity was patronizing. "Don't you know," Monica said, hesitantly, painfully, "—it's impolite to suggest that I'm so much poorer than you are?"

"I don't see that it's either 'impolite' or 'polite,'" Sheila said stiffly. "It happens to be true, doesn't it?"

But if Monica countered by giving Sheila something it was invariably the wrong thing: a pair of hand-knit gloves from Turkey which turned out to be so crudely fashioned that Sheila couldn't force them on her hands, a Scarlatti recording that interested her so little she scarcely glanced at it, and would have left it behind in Monica's kitchen if Monica hadn't called after her. And Monica's most ambitious —and expensive—purchase, a book of photographs of Antarctica by Eliot Porter, must have been similarly unappreciated: Monica noted it lying on a table in Sheila's studio, week after week, always in the same position, untouched.

* * *

Sometimes it happened that though Sheila invited Monica to Edgemont for dinner she found that she couldn't stop work—she needed just another hour, another two hours—but she begged Monica not to go away: she'd be terribly lonely if she went away: couldn't she wander about the house or the property, couldn't she find a quiet place somewhere to read, or even do a little work of her own...? Sheila's nerves were at so high a pitch, her color so flushed, Monica was rather more flattered than hurt: it struck her as extraordinary, that this remarkable woman should have taken an interest in *her*.

She was even responsible—so Sheila said—for "lightening" the tone of one of her canvases, the last in a thematic series she was preparing for a show. "It's your influence—your blond aura," Sheila said. "It really has made a significant difference."

Before Monica visited Sheila's studio for the first time, in early October, she felt a clutch of apprehension. She was worried that she might be forced to lie about Sheila's work—and she knew herself to be, as her husband had called her, an "insultingly unconvincing" liar. But the paintings were most unusual, most striking. There were nine of them, six large triptychs and three smaller canvases, in a style she would have characterized as Abstract, though she knew very little about contemporary art theory. The prejudices she had had before meeting Sheila Trask—the smug little bigotries and affectations—had long since dissolved; she was ashamed to have imagined she knew anything at all. ("But surely you know what you like?" Sheila said, winking, "—or what you suspect you should like?")

Sheila was in the midst of completing the series for a show in late February. She had more than enough time, she said—she wouldn't be caught up in the usual frenzy and anxiety of the final weeks—she wouldn't make the same tactical error she had made the last time. ("What do you mean by the 'last time'? What happened?" Monica asked. "Nothing I want to talk about," Sheila said curtly.) The sequence of paintings had been started years ago, before Morton's death, and afterward she had put the canvases away to work on other things, less ambitious things, simply to keep her mind occupied and her nervous energy flowing so that it wouldn't back up on her. ("If I don't work I get sick, and when I'm sick I can't work—I've never known which comes first," Sheila said.)

Sunshine fell so blindingly through the skylight that Monica had to shield her eyes. She studied the canvases, aware of Sheila's close presence, Sheila's scent, the bright black slightly derisive eyes, the cigarette slanted in the lips, the posture of self-mockery, self-consciousness, apprehension. Monica looked from one canvas to another to another. She felt an instant's sensation of alarm—vertigo. Were the paintings as remarkable as she thought?—as beautiful?—or was her eye simply befuddled by the privilege of the occasion?—Sheila Trask's affection for her, Sheila Trask's intense and unwavering interest in *her*.

Sheila said: "If you're trying to 'like' it, Monica—if you're trying to think of some appropriate adjectives— please don't: I didn't bring you up here for that."

The series was called "Ariadne's Thread." It had to do, Sheila explained, with the idea or memory of a labyrinth, not the actual labyrinth—"in which," Sheila said mysteriously, "we don't always believe." Of the nine canvases only three appeared to be completed and were propped up against the rear wall. The others were ranged haphazardly about the studio, several laid flat on the rather filthy floor. Their colors were muted, subtle—grays shading into mauve, mauve into filmy white—intimations of clouds, a network of nerves, the brain's secret convolutions. A grid of some sort, not altogether geometrical, appeared to be the organizing structure behind the rough-textured surface paints, but it was visible only in patches. Monica, staring, her senses almost too painfully alert, supposed she could see a progression of sorts from the earliest canvas to the last, which was indeed the lightest and the most buoyant of the nine. It was also the least convoluted: did that mean the labyrinth had been overcome—?

Monica murmured a few things—she did like the paintings very much or, at least, she felt disturbed and provoked by them—they seemed to her extraordinary—but of course she couldn't explain—she felt so impoverished— her vocabulary, her emotions—

"Not at all," Sheila said, laying a hand on her arm, *"you're* not the impoverished one."

Sheila stamped out her cigarette in a coffee mug but almost immediately lit another. She mentioned, as if casually, that since Morton's death and since something that had happened to her—to her body—at about that time, she had lost the desire, and most likely the ability as well, to paint subjects head-on. She hadn't the faith, probably, that the subject existed; that her perception of it existed in any absolute way; that its inner being (spiritual, structural) corresponded at all to its surface. "We are all contained inside our bodies—trapped, if you think of it," Sheila said nervously. She felt no contempt, she said, for her fellow artists who counted themselves realists, in fact she envied them, they seemed so young, so untouched, there was something childlike and belligerent in their art. But she could no longer paint that way because she could no longer think that way. Even her eye "thought"—that is, it "saw"—differently.

"Now everything seems to me refracted through mind," Sheila said strangely.

"'Mind'? But why do you say 'mind'?" Monica asked. "Why so general a term, when surely you mean your own—?"

Sheila appeared to be surprised and a little vexed by the question. "No, of course I don't mean my own," she said impatiently, "—of what possible interest would that be to *me?*"

Sheila was much more at ease showing Monica photographs of Morton Flaxman's work—there were pieces by him in virtually every art museum and collection of distinction in the country—and canvases by other artists, many of them friends of her husband's, artists who had come to prominence in the fifties: Milton Avery, Adolph Gottlieb, Hans Hofmann, Franz Kline. Hanging in Sheila's living room, and drawing the eye helplessly to it, was one of de Kooning's "Woman" paintings: so barbaric, so angry, so crazy in its swirls and swaths of paint, Monica laughed aloud in sheer nervousness when she first saw it: "My God, do you live with *that* every day—?" she asked. Sheila, however, said coldly that it was one of the most beautiful paintings ever painted.

One afternoon she took Monica into a storage space below her studio and showed her earlier things she had done herself, sketches, watercolors, oil paintings, everything unframed and much of it, Monica saw with dismay, in battered condition. Some of the work dated back to Sheila's student days at the New York Academy of Art, much of it to the early years of her marriage. Monica flinched as Sheila, squatting awkwardly, pawed through a pile of large, soiled, dog-eared sheets of sketching paper, drawings she had done so long ago, she said, she couldn't remember a single one—horses, trees, outcroppings of rock, uncompleted still lifes, numberless human figures, nude, male and female (including several, Monica thought, of her husband—though perhaps she was mistaken, Sheila paid them so little heed). She drew a forearm roughly across her perspiring face and said she couldn't imagine why she kept so much junk: if she had any shame—if she had enough energy to waste—she would heap these things together and burn them.

Monica was shocked. "But these are extremely interesting things—don't you think they're valuable?"

". . . Geological strata, old dead days, days and weeks and years, in fact," Sheila said, her face flushed. "So much hope and expectation . . . and sheer diligence. . . . Now I'm forced to see these things through your eyes, and my mind is absolutely blank. It's as if a hose had swept everything clean. I don't know what to think—I don't even know what I'm seeing."

"You can't be serious," Monica said warmly. "Anything you do, Sheila—anything you've done—is of value. And some of these things are extremely good."

Sheila squinted up at her, smiling uncertainly. Her heavy eyebrows nearly met above her nose in an expression of quizzical mockery, an expression Monica particularly disliked—it made her friend look ugly.

"Are they?" Sheila said. "But why? Because someone who is well-intentioned says so?—because *you* say so?"

The question was not insolent, Monica realized, or even, coming from Sheila, tactless: it was asked in all sincerity: but how to reply—?

4

GRADUALLY IT CAME about, Monica scarcely knew how, that everyone at the Glenkill Academy knew of her friendship with Sheila Trask. Sheila Trask the painter, Sheila Trask the widow of Morton Flaxman, Sheila Trask who owns—is it Edgemont?—that enormous old house on the Poor Farm Road? If they wondered how, or why, Monica Jensen had been taken up by Sheila Trask, and taken up with such zest (was she an artist herself? had she an interest in art?) they made no inquiries, at least to Monica: their questions were solely about Sheila Trask.

What is she like, what is she *really* like?—is she as eccentric as everyone says? And what does Edgemont look like on the inside?

And why does she drive that beaten-up old station wagon—?

And why, for God's sake, does she dress the way she does—!

Monica made no attempt to disguise her irritation, even with her older colleagues. She told them that Sheila Trask was a "complex" person. And "very private." Trembling with anger, she composed a dignified little speech which, one day in the faculty dining room, she delivered to Brian Farley himself: "Sheila loathes the fact that people here gossip about her, people who know nothing about her—who've never set foot in Edgemont."

Monica would not have minded—she would in fact have felt it a challenge—if they had made inquiries about Sheila's art: what sort of thing was she working on now, did she belong to any "school" or "style," how did Monica respond to it—? But no one, with the exception of Jill Starkie (who "expressed her religious awe of her Maker" by doing watercolors of barns and covered bridges) mentioned the work at all. If they spoke of Sheila Trask in any professional sense it was only to speak of Morton Flaxman, who had been one of the "big names" in the area for years. He had sold work to museums and collections all over the world, he'd been written about in national magazines, been given awards, declined awards, accepted commissions, declined commissions, been mentioned alongside Moore, Calder, Lipchitz, David Smith. . . . He had been controversial in his time; he had been outspoken. There was even an early piece of his, a figure of sorts in stone, aluminum, and bronze, displayed proudly in front of the school library: "Solstice" was its enigmatic name.

Flaxman had been given the imprimatur of a publicized fame, but his wife, his widow, though said to have a decent reputation in the world of art, was an untabulated quantity.

It was rumored that she might have to declare bankruptcy—the entire estate was going to be seized for taxes.

It was rumored that she was making a fortune—and not a small fortune—selling her husband's work.

It was rumored that she would remarry—a much younger man.

(In fact—hadn't he been a protégé of her husband's? Hadn't they been traveling together in the Orient when Flaxman died?)

It was rumored—

But one thing *was* certain, Sheila Trask led a self-destructive life. She had affairs, as everyone knew, with other artists— "people like herself."

Sheila's studio was on the second floor of a converted carriage house set a little distance behind the main house. It was spacious, airy, attractive in its design—the skylight overhead, one wall made of plate glass and brick—but singularly cluttered, *really* messy, to Monica's way of thinking. Painting equipment, old canvases, sheets of newspaper underfoot, dirty cups and plates and silverware, ashtrays unemptied for days, trash cartons unemptied for weeks, soiled articles of clothing and paint-stained towels hanging from the backs of chairs.... The place smelled harshly of paint, turpentine, cigarette smoke, sweat, Sheila's frank undisguised sweat: and fresh-brewed coffee: and something else, something sweet, slightly rancid, which Monica could not define. Though she had been rather shocked by her initial visit to the studio she soon came to like it very much. The mess, the odors, Sheila Trask standing or crouching before one of her canvases... Sheila Trask allowing her entrance, allowing her the privilege of being a witness....

Even her friend's moods interested her. (Sometimes Sheila was excited, almost wildly elated—sometimes she was irritable, angry with herself, contemptuous at the "progress" she was making.) Even the fact, disconcerting at first, that Sheila could ignore her, look through her, forget her for minutes at a time. They might have been old, intimate companions, even sisters.... In the final wretched year of her marriage Monica and her husband had moved through their lives like sleepwalkers, systematically ignoring each other, courteous, cautious, ceaselessly apprehensive. They shared a common space and a span of precisely calibrated time. Monica had not existed for her husband, nor had he existed for her: and by degrees Monica had slipped into a near-perpetual trance of hatred, knowing herself invisible, obliterated, no longer *there*.... But it was different with Sheila Trask. It was entirely different. In fact it seemed to Monica an undeserved privilege, a gift of sorts, that she might be, though physically present, physically forgotten.

But if she sometimes whispered that she'd leave, she'd call a little later that day, Sheila often turned and said: "No. Wait. I'm almost finished." Her voice might be strident and peremptory, it might be almost apologetic, even pleading. "No, wait—I'm almost finished."

Monica thought about Sheila. She thought about "Sheila Trask."

She wanted to be honest with herself—she had always prided herself on being honest, even ruthless, with herself if not with others. What she felt for Sheila Trask was more than simple affection: it had to do with admiration, awe, even—perhaps—envy. (Though envy was not a very attractive impulse. One might more readily confess being filled with sheer hatred, Monica thought, than with envy.) But she could see that Sheila Trask differed significantly from herself and from anyone with whom she had ever been in close contact.

It set her teeth on edge, as Sheila so frequently said, to enter that studio in the morning. It was sheer hell and it was getting worse. She hated the mornings, she hated herself in the mornings, wound up so tight, every muscle quivering, her heartbeat unnaturally rapid, as if she were a child, as if she'd never proved herself at anything! . . . every movement in question, every brush stroke, every decision. Monica asked if Morton Flaxman had been sympathetic with her, if his counsel had helped, and Sheila said, amused, somewhat irritated: "But of course he was the same way—most of the time he was much worse."

She said, grinning, her eyes narrowing slyly: "Most of the time he was crazy and I knew enough to stay out of his way." She was envious, oh yes she was a little jealous, though she couldn't have said why, *could* she have said why?—shaken for hours after a near-quarrel with Sheila one rainy November Sunday, when she discovered the woman working in her drafty studio though she was sick with flu and obviously running a temperature. (In fact her appearance shocked Monica, who hadn't seen her for several days. Eyes bloodshot, lips pale and slack, breasts swaying loose inside a thin cotton T-shirt. And that ravaged skin. And that smell—that rancid smell—of illness.)

Go to bed, Monica advised, call a doctor, better yet let me drive you to a doctor—you have to take care of your health.

Sheila said contemptuously: "What's called 'health' doesn't interest me if nothing is accomplished."

Monica said, with a sharpness that surprised her: "That's a childish attitude. It's a *selfish* attitude."

She *was* slightly jealous, perhaps. But she hid it well.

There was nothing in her life, she came by degrees to see, that corresponded to Sheila's work and to her monomaniacal faith in her work. Even Sheila's marriage, turbulent as it probably had been, was a far more fruitful and significant marriage than Monica's. (She fairly writhed with shame to think of "Harold Bell" set beside "Morton Flaxman." Dear God, if Sheila had ever met Harold—! Self-important and industrious as a bright undergraduate, quick, clever, intermittently "brilliant"—as his professors in Bloomington had praised him—but conventional in imagination, even in ambition. Monica remembered him frowning and squinting at himself in the mirror while shaving, as if he were gravely displeased by what he saw, an ordinarily handsome face, his hair already thinning by the age of twenty-seven, eyes set too close together. "Do you think my eyes are set too close together?" he had asked Monica once, in an odd, vulnerable mood, and Monica had said, amused, "Of course not—what a peculiar thing to ask.")

Sheila's passion, Sheila's mercurial moods. . . . Nothing

in Monica's life corresponded: nothing that was *Jensen* made any claim for the extraordinary. Yet Sheila queried her, nearly interrogated her, what sort of childhood had she had, was her family religious, what was it like to grow up in Wrightsville, Indiana, what was her first experience with death?—with sex? And how had she known she was "in love" with the man she eventually married? (Monica drew her forefinger unconsciously along her jaw, stroking the scar, thinking, thinking very hard, feeling her cheeks burn with the incongruity of her friend's interest and her own meager resources. She heard herself saying things she wasn't certain were altogether true: yes she had thought her body ugly in early adolescence, yes she had been frightened and humiliated by menstruation, yes she had feared she might bleed to death. . . . Yes she did sometimes think of madness: doesn't everyone? And death. Madness and death. Doesn't everyone?)

Monica knew secretly that her capacity for love—for love and what is meant by "passion"—was deficient set beside Sheila Trask's; she knew that Sheila was exaggerating her warmth, her good nature, her "blond optimism"— the attributes, mysterious and somewhat patronizing, she claimed to find in Monica. Was it flattering, or was it subtly comical, that Sheila Trask of all persons should regard her with awe simply because she navigated a day—a not atypical day—of classes, committee meetings, conferences with students, an obligatory coffee hour in the headmaster's residence, and so forth: while Sheila had spent these hours in her studio staring at one canvas after another, seeing no connection between them, no logical relationship, visited by no impulse to work, overcome by a sensation of melancholy and paralysis. At such times, Sheila said, she believed she might be on the planet Jupiter: the gravity so much more powerful, murderous.

"You should remember that I'm paid for what I do,"

Monica said. "I enjoy it—it *is* hard work—but the day consumes itself, almost without my volition—and in any case I wouldn't be there if I weren't being paid."

"Don't you think I'm paid too, eventually?" Sheila said, irritated. "Whatever I *do* at this point in my 'career,' it's something Trask has *done*—which makes the predicament all the more awful. The gravity."

"I don't understand," Monica said, perhaps too lightly.

"Then you *don't*," Sheila said, letting the subject drop.

Monica told herself that she wasn't jealous—well, perhaps she was *slightly* jealous—of Sheila Trask's talent.

And her reputation.

(Monica spent some surreptitious hours in the public library tracking down the elusive artist "Sheila Trask." Browsing through back issues of *Art News, Art in America, American Artist*. Turning the pages of these glossy magazines, examining the illustrations and advertisements, Monica felt her old prejudices return in a flood of mild revulsion. Perhaps it was not the art that offended her so much as the seriousness with which it was presented, and the value—clearly monetary—assigned it. Coils of rope on a gallery floor; ungainly white plaster figures of "humanoid" design; black stripes on boards; smashed crockery; American flags dipped in paint; a massive coil of chicken wire; "Action Painting"; "assemblage sculpture"; "Pop Art." She stared at photographs of a middle-aged male artist who had systematically burnt himself with cigarettes and made odd little nicks in his skin with a knife— and very subdued and proud the man appeared, as the herald of a "new and revolutionary" approach to art. There was the media-celebrated artist who had "packaged" several Miami islands in fluorescent-pink plastic, and another artist, scarcely less celebrated, who had publicized the idea—simply the idea—of packaging the entire globe in a similar material. . . . In this context it did not surprise Monica to learn that Sheila Trask with her nonrepresentational but highly detailed canvases was considered a "conservative," even a "traditionalist." Her work was described as Abstract Expressionism of a sort, in its "lyric" phase; yet it was related too to Minimalism; even to Primary Structuralism—whatever that meant: Monica gathered that it had something to do with sculpture. Trask's work was "ascetic" . . . and "hedonistic" . . . and "cerebral" . . . and "impulsive." It quite clearly derived from Cubism; yet there was an element of Action Painting in it, and overtones of German Expressionism. A predecessor was Hans Hofmann—unless it was de Kooning—and of course the influence of Morton Flaxman was never to be underestimated. One lengthy article in *American Artist* included a photograph of Trask's studio in which Sheila Trask—somber, down-looking, very young and very thin—stood with her hands in her coverall pockets between two immense paintings propped against a wall; and it seemed to Monica that Sheila Trask herself was far more interesting than her work. Those large canvases, those queer unsettling strands and loops and stains of color, those empty areas—what was one to make of them? what words would do?)

Of course Monica took pride in *her* work as well. Yet she hardly wanted to become self-righteous about it: teaching at the Glenkill Academy was not quite like teaching in the South Bronx, for instance, where one's capacity for inventiveness and energy and moral courage might be tested to the full. Week by week, however, she was becoming more confident; it might be said—perhaps soon it would be said—that Miss Jensen was one of the "popular" teachers. Her students had seemed mistrustful of her at first (because she was a woman?—she rather hoped that was all) but now they were relaxed and congenial, they laughed at her humorous remarks, they appeared to respect her, they *were* working hard at her assignments and quite clearly learning something. As for the Glenkill community, the adults—they too seemed to like Monica well enough. Even, perhaps, a little more than that.

(Should popularity matter so much, even in adulthood? Monica worried. But it was a matter of her job, after all.)

It was Sheila's belief that most people were fraudulent, hypocritical, shallow, inconsequential. Their souls—as she was fond of saying—were no deeper than dime-store teaspoons. (Hearing this odd remark for the third or fourth time, Monica had wanted to ask whether silver-plated teaspoons were "deeper" than dime-store teaspoons.) Most people, Sheila said, move from one superficial experience to another and prattle about "experience" and what it meant to them; they take up one interest after another; one occupation or preoccupation. But nothing really touches them —they can't be *hurt*. "It's possible to feel affection for such people," Sheila said, "but you can't really be friends with them—the bond doesn't go deeply enough. Somehow you can't believe in their existence. They're expendable. They don't matter."

Monica thought, chilled: She's talking about me. But does she know it?

One very dark night when Sheila was driving Monica home along the Olcottsville Road, Monica said suddenly: "You think the capacity to be hurt—to be betrayed and hurt—is a sign of depth? Of seriousness?"

Sheila was driving rather fast considering the narrow road's numerous curves and the faulty condition of the station wagon's brakes, about which she often complained. She said, vague, distracted: "—of death? What?—I didn't hear."

5

ONE AFTERNOON, HAVING volunteered to sort through an accumulation of years' work ("work and rubbish," as Sheila said) in the vast closet in Sheila's studio, Monica discovered, unframed, an exquisite little watercolor of a winter scene—a "realistic" winter scene. She even recognized the setting, a few miles down the Poor Farm Road, where the ruins of the old poor farm were visible from the road amidst a stand of scrub pine. How beautiful the painting was! How delicate! Her hand trembled faintly as she brought it, in triumph, to show to Sheila.

"That? What the hell is *that?"* Sheila said, squinting. There was no date on the painting, no signature or initials. But, surely, it was her own work: and she supposed that Monica could have it if she really wanted it and if she didn't go out of her way to say who had painted it. "Such a *pretty* landscape," she said jeeringly, "—but wintry and craggy too: see that outcropping of rock? Almost as good as Andrew or Jamie Wyeth."

Monica said defensively that she did think the painting was beautiful. And it was certainly worth a great deal of money, so she couldn't accept it as a present. She had hoped Sheila might sell it to her. . . .

"For Christ's sake," Sheila said, snorting in amusement, "don't take that tone with me. Please. I mean *don't.* If you like it, and if you have the wall space, take it, take it and shut up, see if you can find a decent frame somewhere and I'll frame it, the transaction will take four and a half minutes and that's that. It *isn't* really worth discussing."

Monica repeated that she wanted to buy it. She hadn't at

52

all meant to angle to be given it: she was a professional woman just as Sheila was a professional woman. And it was an article of faith of hers that—

"I said don't take that tone, please," Sheila said, though less amused now, "—it's abrasive, it's pompous, it isn't necessary. You found it and it's yours."

"But Sheila—"

"Otherwise I'll rip it up: do you want me to rip it up?"

"I don't think you're being reasonable. I had wanted—"

"Look, it's pointless to argue. I don't argue. I'm busy at the moment and I don't have time to argue and the main thing is—I'd actually be very happy to see the painting hanging in your house, if you really like it, if it *really* appeals to you," Sheila said. "Here, it doesn't exist. It has no value. But I suppose it could have another life of sorts with you."

Monica's senses were sharpened, her pulsebeat quick, agitated, still combative. How bullying Sheila was!—how purely insufferable, in her self-conceit! But Monica backed down. She said, faltering: "But—are you sure? I mean— I hadn't intended— It really is so beautiful—"

Sheila too relented, suddenly. She examined the slightly tattered watercolor from a distance of several feet, her head turned to the side as if she couldn't force herself to consider it directly. "Well—you'd say it was 'beautiful'? In your eyes it's 'beautiful'?" She stared, she screwed up her face, ran her tongue fiercely across her front teeth. "Jesus, I wish I cared about that kind of thing now. That beauty. That delicacy. I wish I could even see it."

Monica took away the watercolor as if she feared her friend's simple presence might do injury to it. She spent some minutes hunting down a suitable frame, feeling wonderfully triumphant, elated. *Had* she been angling to be given the painting, after all?—had it all been some sort of game, a pretense, not only her own high moral tone but

Sheila's initial contempt? But no—Sheila had come close to snatching the watercolor out of her fingers and tearing it in two. But *yes*—that would have been part of the game, that violence. And Monica's scream of protest.

Afterward she said: "But, Sheila, it isn't fair—what can I give you in return? I don't have anything of value—I don't have anything you want."

The remark hung awkwardly between them. Monica had spoken without thinking—warmly, impetuously, uncharacteristically—and there was nothing Sheila could say. Yet she *couldn't* remain silent because her silence would be an insult. So she murmured, finally, embarrassed: "Friendship isn't a matter of barter, is it?"

6

"THE ONLY eccentric thing about her," Monica said stiffly, the next time she was asked about Sheila Trask, "—is her generosity. I've never known anyone like her."

7

ARIADNE'S THREAD: the labyrinth as a state of mind, a region of the soul: heroic effort without any Hero at its center. ("This is only about Ariadne's thread, this has nothing to do with Theseus," Sheila said angrily.)

Monica stared, Monica stared hard, but the shifting angles and planes of paint, the subtle gradations of color, conformed to a structural grid she could not quite understand. She felt its logic—its inner sense. Or told herself she did.

But one day she made a mistake. A real blunder. Speaking warmly and effusively, chattering away as, in the past, Sheila had seemed to like her to chatter, she happened to say, "Why don't you stop right at this point, don't do another thing,"—indicating a triptych on which Sheila had been working for the past several days. And Sheila had gone white with rage. She had barely been able to speak.

Monica sensed her tactlessness—her frank stupidity—at once; and hurriedly backed down. Of course Sheila knew what she was doing, what she wanted, Monica knew nothing, Monica was being intrusive and idiotic and was very, very sorry.

Afterward she asked Sheila shyly whether she had really been so angry as she'd appeared.

Sheila said: "Don't ever tempt me. Don't. Don't."

Monica began to acquire an appetite for her friend's studio. That place of strain and tension and raw nerves. That place of sudden laughter, fresh-brewed coffee, Danish pastry devoured ravenously—Sheila's hands trembling because she hadn't eaten in a very long time: and Monica proved her "angel of mercy." ("But how can you go without eating for so long?" Monica asked, mystified. "Do you simply forget?—does your body allow you to forget?")

Sheila Trask's studio, that place of exuberant high spirits, that place of secrecy and refuge . . . Sheila had a telephone but it was nearly always unplugged. (Sometimes, late at night, she plugged it in, she said, so that she could dial to learn what time it was! . . . she didn't allow any clock or watch in the studio.) The main house was kept in a reasonable state of cleanliness by Sheila's housekeeper and one or two cleaning women who came out once a week; there were a few groundsmen and handymen, irregularly employed; and a teenaged boy came over from a neighboring farm to help out with Sheila's three horses. But none of these people ever approached the carriage house. And even when she knew she was expected, Monica often felt an unreasonable sense of trespass, almost of danger, as she ascended the stairs.

For what if the door were locked against her? And Sheila, though inside, refused to open it—?

Monica acquired an appetite for the harsh astringent odors of paint and turpentine, she imagined they cleared her head, made her eyes water so that her vision came more sharply into focus. She no longer minded the filthy rags underfoot, the torn newspapers, shards of broken crockery, an old sweater of Sheila's stiff with dirt which had been lying beside a chair for weeks. And the constantly varying—the *unpredictably* varying—degrees of light from the skylight fascinated her. She theorized that all romance is *light*—light's gentle diminution, light's raw intensity. Sheila Trask standing exposed in the pitiless white light of a winter noontide was not a beautiful woman—age showed shockingly in her face, even in the lusterless frizzy aureole of her hair. But Sheila Trask standing in the slow-fading light of an overcast afternoon possessed (how suddenly!—how totally without her knowledge) a solemn ascetic beauty Monica found enthralling.

Ariadne's thread held tightly, prayerfully, in the fingers. The labyrinth as a state of mind, a permanent state of mind. Monica wandered in it, utterly content.

But the secrets were all Sheila's. Sheila held herself rigid and surrendered nothing. Smiles came unbidden, laughter was sudden and sometimes a little shrill, excluding Monica. Sheila boasted that her life—like her very body—existed at a distance from her. It was *hers,* but not *her.*

Monica laughed uneasily, pretending to understand. ("What did you mean, Sheila, when you said that something had happened to you—to your body—around the time of your husband's death?—and that your attitude toward painting changed afterward?" she asked. And Sheila replied without expression, carefully: "When did I ever tell you that?"—and a moment later added: "That's bullshit.")

But she was insensitive, even ruthless, about Monica's private life. In fact it came to seem, as time passed, that Monica's past was a possession or privilege of Sheila's, to be dissected and analyzed at length. Especially if the hour was late. Especially if Sheila's work had not gone well that day. If they were alone together in Monica's living room with a fire burning—an apple-wood fire Sheila had provided, and kept going—or in Sheila's country kitchen, white stucco walls and blue and white ceramic tile, copper utensils hanging from a rack, a near-depleted bottle of red wine on the table between them. It might be twenty after twelve, it might be five minutes to one, Sheila restless and impatient and provoking because she'd had too much to drink, Monica herself a little drunk, surprising herself by speaking in a voice she didn't always recognize. It was an oddity of these visits—she would always remember it— that Sheila's Irish setter Siegmund would wriggle by inches across the kitchen floor and come to rest, lightly wheezing, with his heavy head on Monica's foot. ("Are you sure you don't mind?" Sheila asked doubtfully. "He's almost twelve years old—he's lonely, he's affectionate—very sweet— but sometimes rather tiresome. Do you see those eyes?— more human than *mine*.")

Sheila asked questions but (so Monica told herself) she wasn't prying. She was simply a friend who was very interested in Monica and wasn't it flattering, to know oneself a subject of interest?—when life was so comfortable and routine otherwise.

Tell me about your marriage, Sheila would urge, lighting a cigarette and watching her closely, pitilessly,—tell me why you want to dismiss it as a "mistake." Why you don't want to take responsibility for it. Why you imagine you have walked away free.

Monica laughed and pressed the backs of her hands against her face. Was she drunk? So warm, so warmly befuddled? She felt no danger. Well—perhaps she felt some danger. She spoke of her marriage as if it had happened to another person, a fool, a deserving victim, a very young woman. She should have known: Harold had been so amusing in his contempt for homely women, or unkempt women, or women who wore too much makeup, or women whose legs or underarms were stubbled and not smoothly shaven. An affront to him. Yes clearly: an affront to any man who chanced to look in their direction.

"But now you're free," Sheila said. There was a nudge of irony in her voice but her dark eyes were fixed compassionately on Monica's face.

"I'm free," Monica said lightly. "I'm living in a place in

Pennsylvania I didn't know existed a year ago."

"And are you happy?" Sheila asked.

"I'm happy," Monica said, again lightly. "I'm very happy."

"Do you know why?" Sheila asked, watching her closely.

Monica drained her glass. Her voice was brave though faintly trembling. "Because I'm here," she said. "In Glenkill. In my own life. My name is Jensen again—it was always Jensen. I don't need to care whether I have a 'husband'—whether he's faithful or unfaithful—whether he loves me too much—as he thought at one point he did—or doesn't love me at all—"

Sheila interrupted to ask whether Monica's husband had actually been unfaithful to her; and, really, why had it mattered? "Men are always unfaithful to women in one way or another," Sheila said.

"Did you feel that way when your husband was unfaithful to you?" Monica asked sharply.

Sheila shrugged her shoulders. She smiled and showed her damp predator's teeth. "I don't remember," she said.

Monica told herself she should leave: it was time to go home: it was past the time to go home: she'd feel wretched in the morning. But she stayed. The Irish setter's chin resting on her foot was so warm, so comforting, her head ached half-pleasantly, a low dull throbbing at the base of her skull. She stayed until two, two-ten, two-twenty. A freezing rain had begun, pelting the windows. She found herself speaking rapidly and a little crazily about her marriage. Yes it had been this, yes she'd told herself it was that, no she had been lying, yes she *had* been lying, the secrets were so clumsy, so obvious, why was she crying?—making a fool of herself?—drunk and maudlin as her husband had always detested in women: and of course her soul was as shallow as a tin spoon. Sheila had seen through her at once, Sheila couldn't be deceived. . . . She heard herself saying that her marriage had been doomed because it hadn't been blessed—there was such a thing as "blessed"—she didn't know how to explain and she wasn't religious any longer but she did believe—didn't Sheila?—that some relationships were blessed and others were cursed. And you always know, Monica declared, her voice slurred, you *always* know.

Then she was speaking of blessings and curses. And the strain of keeping a delusion intact: "All your strength goes into it, it's like the first twelve weeks of a pregnancy, the new life feeding off yours. . . ." Then she was crying again. Or she had been crying all along, rubbing her fist into her eye as she'd seen Sheila do, as she had done as a child. Her nose running and her cheeks hot and damp and her throat constricted with pain. He had made her have the abortion, she said. No he had only wanted her to have the abortion, it had been his *wish*. She couldn't see how she was to blame but he blamed her. But she was to blame. He knew. He guessed. The stratagem was hers, the trick. To get pregnant, to make a change in their lives, to force the issue. *I will force the issue,* she had thought, manic with excitement. Then, afterward, the guilt—the luxury of guilt—sucking and gnawing on guilt—Monica weeping hysterically in Harold's arms because they were murderers because they were trapped together in an act of supreme significance because it was all a ruse and Monica was play-acting Monica hadn't loved him from the start Monica hadn't been capable of love but had quite liked being loved. "It was really all my fault," she said, "—but the sympathy was for me: he had 'made' me have an abortion and then he 'stopped loving' me."

She was shamefaced, crying, laughing in surprised

hiccuping gulps, she hadn't known until this moment, Sheila staring at her, Sheila leaning forward staring at her, what a liar she was: and how perceptive her husband had been, to know. Even as she wept. Even as she coiled upon herself wanting to die. Near the end she claimed that she loved him after all and he said, "That's a mistake, then, *don't*," then shortly afterward he said, "No, you're lying again," and she had thought her heart might be wrenched out of her body. It was as if the embryonic life—*her* life—had been sucked out of her body a second time.

She wept, hugging herself. Her breasts were aching, her belly, her loins. After a moment Sheila reached out and touched the scar on Monica's jaw, one tentative forefinger, direct, not especially gentle. "Did he have anything to do with this—I've always wondered."

Monica drew away at once.

No, it had been an accident.

A hot blush rose from her throat: it had been an accident.

—They were quarreling and he must have shoved her— half-sobbing himself, furious, exhausted—he shoved her and she stumbled and fell and struck her jaw on the sharp edge of a counter—no it hadn't been deliberate—not entirely deliberate— the pain was remarkable—the pain was a stroke of lightning—and he was as appalled as she: blood streaming down her throat and chest, soaking into her clothes. They weren't the sort of people who did such things.

She couldn't stop crying. Sheila rose without a word and stooping, cradled Monica's head in her arms, rocked her slightly, comforted her. Monica was utterly helpless, she couldn't have said where she was, weeping, clutching at someone, a presence, a strength, so much superior to her own. She smelled tobacco and wine and stale perspiration

—a muscular warmth—merging with the old stench of panic and blood, the ache along her jaw, memory stitched in flesh.

Afterward she thought, not knowing whether to be ashamed: Of course Sheila knew about the scar all along.

PART II

———◆———

The Mirror-Ghoul

1

"WHO ARE HER friends, Monica?—I mean besides you," Jill Starkie asked one evening at dinner, at the Starkies' house on the Academy campus. She was wearing a kind of Japanese kimono that opened slightly as she leaned forward, releasing a sweet earnest scent of lilies of the valley. As the evening's hostess she had been smiling for some time and now her pink-glossed lips were bracketed by ghostly smiles. When Monica stared at the tablecloth before her—she'd been making faint indentations in the Irish linen with her fork—and could not seem to think of an adequate reply, Jill said, persisting, leaning farther forward: "But she *has* friends, hasn't she? I mean—besides you."

"Of course she has friends," Monica said. But her mind had gone blank: she could think of a half-dozen persons whom she had met at Edgemont, casually and very informally; she recalled Sheila mentioning the names of friends in New York and Key West and Mexico and the Costa del Sol and Morocco—friends, fellow artists, companions of her late husband's. But none of the names came to mind as Jill Starkie and the others at the table looked at her, waiting.

"There used to be odd stories about her, lovers of hers who turned up at the wrong time," another guest at the table said, "if we're talking about the same woman: Morton Flaxman's widow?"

"Sheila *Trask*," Jill said in a tone of light, animated reproach. "You must know her name, David, she's nearly as accomplished as her husband, in fact I prefer her work—

don't make a face, Brian, I *do*—what I've seen of it, I mean—*his* is so overbearing and monolithic, if that's the word—so aggressively monumental—*and* so overpriced —"

At this point James Starkie interrupted helpfully to say, in a slightly too-hearty voice, that Monica was a friend of Sheila Trask's.

"Yes, Monica has become friendly with Sheila Trask," Jill repeated, speaking a little breathlessly. Her nervous fingers fluttered at her throat and an enormous stone, a diamond?—a zircon?—winked and gleamed on her right hand. "So we were thinking—I mean, I was thinking— just the other day—I haven't had time to speak with you about this, Monica—but I was thinking it would be an excellent opportunity—I mean for Glenkill—for the school—to invite her over to speak to the boys, the boys who are interested in art—and we could all have dinner together—here, or at the Greenes'—I *know* Harry and Ruth would be delighted." She paused for the briefest of moments but only to draw breath. ". . . Some of you remember when Morton Flaxman visited?—a long time ago —James and I were very new—Mr. Flaxman gave a marvelous lecture—a kind of free-association talk—he had a wonderful sense of humor—salty and profound—of course he *did* drink a bit—but he was really a genius, as everyone says—so much energy and enthusiasm and expertise—though, as I say, I think his work is a bit over-rated—and certainly overpriced. Some of us couldn't *believe* what the trustees paid him for that piece by the library!—of course it was commissioned—and I suppose it was very special—but, still—prices in the art world are so astronomical, I suppose. I wonder if Sheila Trask commands that sort of fee? I suppose not—considering she's younger—and a woman. It would be fascinating to hear her speak and to become acquainted with her, wouldn't it?

I don't believe she came along with her husband that evening," Jill said, glancing at her husband, frowning, "—no, I'm certain she didn't. The Greenes invited her, of course, but for some reason she didn't come."

Monica felt obliged to speak, to defend her friend. But for some reason—a minute streak of malice, perhaps?— she said nothing. She was making crosshatched indentations in the tablecloth with her dessert fork.

"They're all a bit reclusive, the artists we've known," James Starkie said. "Even the artists who've taught here. You have to respect that—it's part of their nature. *I* respect that."

"I respect it too, James," Jill said quickly, "but Sheila Trask lives so close by, it's a pity not to draw upon her. If she met our students and saw how bright they are, how talented, and how sweet—*aren't* they sweet, some of them?—I know she'd be impressed. Do you think you might bring up the subject to her, Monica?—for sometime after the Christmas break?"

"Sheila has a new show in February," Monica said. "I really don't think she'd have time to visit us."

"Then *after* February, of course," Jill said, smiling at Monica as if Monica had said something particularly obtuse. "There's all the time in the world and I know Harry and Ruth would be delighted. . . ."

Monica felt the prick, the lightest pinprick, of coercion. But she only murmured a vague reply, neutral and near-inaudible.

James said with a droll smile that the artists he and Jill had known—and they'd known quite a few, beginning back in college—this was in Columbus, Ohio—Ohio State, where they'd met—the artists they had known were really colorful and eccentric personalities—unpredictable —rather childlike, in fact. Difficult to get along with but sometimes very likable. Lovable. "It never surprised me,"

James said expansively, "the things we'd hear from time to time about the Flaxmans, and it never made me feel there was anything, you know, immoral about them. They simply abide by a different set of standards than the rest of us, and in God's creation each individual only has to account for himself—no matter what the Pharisees preach."

James Starkie was a burly good-natured man in his early forties who looked and behaved like a man in his late twenties. At Ohio State he had been a football star—so Monica had been told, many times—and it was considered quite a coup for Glenkill, that their much-admired chaplain was an athlete and a companion of young athletes, his name well-known to alumni. All the boys adored him, it was said—or nearly all: perhaps his relentless good nature and his white-toothed smile failed to charm the more "problematic" of the boys.

Monica liked him. She wanted to like him. She could see clearly that both James Starkie and his wife were genuine Christians, forthright, sunny, not at all hypocritical, possessed of the good news of salvation, the Good News of the Gospels—they were old-fashioned, unembarrassed, the real thing. Certainly they meant well. They meant *good*. And if she hadn't Sheila Trask she would have been grateful for their frequent invitations to dinner and their general solicitude. (Early in the fall Jill had invited her to lunch to tell her that she shouldn't worry about being lonely in Glenkill because it was impossible to be lonely— the Glenkill faculty and students were all one family. "I mean we really *are*," Jill said. "It's only that new instructors sometimes feel a little left out—excluded—simply because they're new to the family, and worried, you know, worried—" here she flailed about for a moment, clearly in awkward waters, "—about being kept on, that sort of thing. But it's just because they're new." She had reached out to squeeze Monica's hand, as if impulsively; she was

eaning so close, and smiling so happily, Monica halfway
worried that she would suddenly embrace her. But she only
said: "I know that won't be the case with you, Maura, I
mean *Monica,* because you're basically not the type at all,
 mean to be excluded and lonely, to stand off to the side
making critical judgments; you're more like me—I could
see from the first that you're more like me.")

Monica was hoping that the subject of Sheila Trask
would be dropped but Brian Farley, the chairman of her
department, persisted. He was a bull-necked solid man in
his midfifties, handsome in a somewhat pocked and battered way, known on campus for his wit, his "remarkable
erudition," his admiration for Evelyn Waugh. He sometimes affected a slightly British drawl and he had begun to
resemble Waugh about the eyes. He asked Monica point-
edly what Edgemont looked like on the inside: was Sheila
Trask keeping things up, or letting things go, as rumor had
it?—after all, the woman had a certain responsibility as
"mistress" of a house like that.

Monica said quietly that she wasn't a judge of such
matters but so far as she knew Edgemont was in excellent
condition. Of course Sheila had her own work, her ener-
gies were channeled almost exclusively into her own
work—"she isn't a museum curator, after all, or the priest-
ess at a shrine."

Farley replied with a semblance of affability that he had
always admired Morton Flaxman's work—it was strong,
unsentimental, unmannered. As for Sheila Trask's "work"
—he'd seen a feature on her in one of the newsmagazines
—*Time,* or *Newsweek,* he couldn't remember—this must
have been five years ago—and he didn't know whether to
be appalled or amused by the attention paid to such trash.
All swirls and wildness and arbitrary color, no coherence to
it, another joke played on the public—"the insatiably *asi-
nine* public"—as comical as, what were their names,

Jasper Johns?—Pollock?—and the Frenchman who assembled collages out of garbage dumps—what *was* his name—

The Starkies' guests laughed though they were rather embarrassed for Monica. Jill shook a scolding forefinger at Farley and told him that he just didn't *understand,* he hadn't made any effort, had he?—to *understand?*

Farley continued in the same falsely amiable tone, speaking, it seemed, to Monica; he said he'd heard rather remarkable things about her friend. It was commonly known that she took drugs—amphetamines; she was a binge drinker; probably an alcoholic. She'd been known to show up at country taverns unescorted, as far away as Edgarsville and Bethany. She formed "passionate attachments" to women and men both, sometimes very young men, painters, and all sorts of odd things happened. . . . Then there was the famous Dorr case, Farley said, now smiling broadly, the man had been having an affair with Sheila Trask, or the woman—the wife—that actress with all the red hair?—she'd been having an affair with Flaxman and one night they tried to kill each other—he didn't have the details quite in order but he remembered that the Dorr woman had shot her husband's ear off with his own revolver—and afterward they'd tried to blame it on a burglar?—wasn't that the story?—

Farley appeared to be asking Monica so she said, stiffly, barely able to control her hatred of him: "I really wouldn't know. I've only lived in the house since September."

Farley clapped his hand to his forehead in what seemed to be a genuine expression of surprise; and even some regret. "I'd forgotten that you live in the Dorrs' old house," he said, in an apologetic voice. He really did seem quite embarrassed suddenly. "Well—it's just a story," he said, glancing up and down the table at his audience, "—just a local legend, I wouldn't want to swear to the truth of any

of it. Or even," he said, with an abrupt puckish grin,
'—that it was the gentleman's *ear* that was shot off. That
may well have been a euphemism for a more offensive
member."

That night, undressing in her rather chilly bedroom, with a
single light burning, Monica caught sight of her wavering
image in the bureau mirror and wondered that it was so
altered. Her fading "golden" hair now looked bleached of
all color; her eyes were unnaturally bright; her face was
flushed, animated—as beautiful as it had ever been. And
there was no one to see.

Her color was so high, she supposed, her eyes so glit-
tering, because she was still trembling with rage. She
wanted to telephone Sheila to warn her—she wanted to
protect her, commiserate with her, how she hated such people, such petty smirking envious people!—Farley with his
smug bulldog face and British drawl—Farley who had
seemed for the first time in their acquaintance an enemy of
hers, of hers and Sheila's—

She lay in bed, sleepless, wretched, hearing again the
prattle at the dinner table, hearing Farley's mocking voice
and her own thin cold reply. Had she betrayed Sheila, she
wondered, by speaking so calmly?—so without passion?
Without telling them how contemptible they all were—
how irremediably shallow—set beside a woman like
Sheila Trask?

She found herself stroking the invisible scar. For comfort, perhaps. For angry solace. It seemed to leap to her
fingertips, pulsing warmly, hotly, stitched like memory into
her flesh, a delicious secret. Though it was, she remembered, no longer a secret, strictly speaking.

2

AND SUDDENLY, IN the first week of December, there was a mystery—a minor mystery—puzzling rather than frightening—in her life: someone had been "making inquiries" about her in Glenkill. A man of no particular age, no distinctive features, soft-voiced, unemphatic, discreet in his questions and even more discreet in giving explanations of his own. The drugstore, the grocery store, the variety store, even the real estate agency—even the Glenkill Academy!—he'd managed to visit them all, asking for information about Miss Monica Jensen.

"But what sort of questions did he ask?" Monica demanded. "—Who could it have been? What did he look like? What did you tell him?"

On all sides Monica was assured, perhaps too vigorously, that of course the man had been told nothing.

Dazed, sickened, Monica had a vision of her former husband in a state of breakdown, turned suddenly against her; spying on her; hoping to ruin her new life. It was unbelievable, but who else cared enough about her to visit Glenkill . . .? To question people about her? Yet Harold had seemed to feel little emotion for her, just as, at the end, she felt such little emotion for him. Their last telephone exchange, months ago, had been brief, perfunctory, even hurried; not at all embittered. "Good-bye," Harold had said, and Monica had said, "Good-bye," and that was that —eight years put to rest.

The headmaster's assistant was an impeccably tailored and well-groomed young man of approximately Monica's age, who spoke confidentially to Monica, yet with some little embarrassment, about the unidentified man who had been asking about her. "He was a private investigator, Miss Jensen—I knew that immediately," he said. "But please be assured, no one cooperated with him. We never do, with people like that."

A private investigator?—a private *detective?* Monica stared, unable to speak for what seemed a very long time.

"He said—or, rather, hinted—just barely hinted—that he was a government agent of some kind, Internal Revenue, maybe—but he had no credentials to show, no badge, it was all a sham," the headmaster's assistant said. Clearly, he felt sorry for Monica, but the sordidness of the situation did not escape him. "In any case, Miss Jensen, we didn't cooperate. When these things happen—occasionally a boy's father will try to investigate him, if there has been a divorce, if there's a child custody suit—when these things happen, no one cooperates; it's Mr. Greene's customary procedure."

But Monica was still staring, speechless.

She began to apologize. She couldn't understand, she said, why anyone would be interested in her—*that* interested!—but she was sorry, very sorry, and rather ashamed, and she hoped he would explain to Mr. Greene—if he thought Mr. Greene might be upset—

"Not at all," the young man said, a trifle stiffly, bringing the interview to an end, "—it isn't necessary for *you* to apologize. As I said, when these things happen no one at the school or in the community cooperates; it's Glenkill policy."

". . . policy?" Monica said faintly.

Monica would have telephoned Sheila with the news, the amazing incredible sickening news, but Sheila was away in Washington on what she called "Flaxman business" (selling art? making arrangements for a museum or gallery exhibit of her late husband's work?—Sheila was always rather oblique) and by the time she returned Monica had decided against telling her. It *was* sickening, it *was* sordid. And there was something unhealthy too about the thrill of self-importance the episode gave Monica.

After all, as everyone insisted, the "investigator" had been told nothing.

On the very day of Sheila's return from Washington Monica happened to receive a letter, at school, from her husband.

There it was, in her mailbox—a quite ordinary and innocent-appearing letter in a plain white envelope, *Harold Bell* typed out neatly above the return address; all very explicit; no subterfuge about it. Surely a letter sent in such a way contained no madness, no accusations or threats . . .? But, seeing it, Monica felt frightened; and thrust it into her handbag at once, as if fearful that someone was watching. Receiving a letter from such a man seemed almost a kind of complicity.

She would open it later, she told herself, when she felt a little stronger.

In the end, however, there was no need for Monica to open the letter at all: Sheila spared her.

Monica gave it to her, explaining that she felt too weak, too shaky, to hear from Harold at the present time. "I don't want to read what he has to say to me, yet I don't want to throw it away," Monica said, her voice trembling. She looked at Sheila with a queer faint hopeful smile. They were seated across from each other in their usual booth in the Chinese restaurant; Sheila was pouring their tea. "I don't dare throw it away," Monica said.

"But I feel like a voyeur, opening it," Sheila said, frowning.

Monica pressed her cool hands against her face to calm

herself. The subtle perfumy scent of the tea both pleased and excited her. She said: "My predicament is, I don't want to read it and I don't want to throw it away without reading it. . . ."

Sheila turned the envelope in her fingers. She said: "The odd thing is, I wanted to write you a letter from Washington. From this dismal antiseptic overpriced hotel in Washington. I wanted to write you a long, long letter . . . but it terrified me, you know, that if I began I wouldn't be able to stop . . . and I'm not good at writing, my nature is too crude and blunt for language. So I didn't write to you, Monica; and now I see that someone else did."

"What were you going to write to me?" Monica asked, surprised.

"How would I know?—if I had written," Sheila said, licking her lips nervously, "I'd know: doing is knowing, after all." She turned the envelope again in her fingers as if weighing it; then, almost impulsively, she ripped it open; skimmed the letter; her eyes narrowed, a flicker of something like distaste, or repugnance, passing over her face. "Nothing," she said in a neutral voice. Then, before Monica could draw breath to speak (she really was frightened, her breath came quick and shallow), Sheila added quickly: "But I see no reason for you to read it, Monica. Certain words, once heard, or read, insinuate themselves in our memories forever; it becomes impossible to dislodge them."

Carefully, yet unobtrusively, as if she were performing a private little ceremony, Sheila tore Harold's letter into several pieces. And Monica, watching, felt an extraordinary sensation of relief and pain—and hilarity as well—as if the tearing sounds had something to do with her nerves, her very soul.

The remainder of the meal, the evening, was characterized by a good deal of laughter and frivolity. Sheila told marvelous serio-comic stories about Washington, Monica interrupted with childish comments and breathless laughter. If only, Monica thought, the evening could go on, and on . . .

3

MONICA WONDERED WHAT Harold's letter had contained. Still more, she wondered what Sheila's letter would have contained.

Now it began to seem that Sheila was absent from her studio more often; that she was markedly less absorbed in her work, and unwilling to talk about it. What she did talk about was fragmentary and jumbled. One day she said contemptuously that money engenders money—"the wheels keep on turning, ever more frantically, after you die"—but the next day she spoke of financial worries, her old anxieties, redoubled. Evidently (so Monica gathered) there was another tax audit. Or a gallery owner was suspected (by Sheila? by Sheila's lawyer?) of cheating her. Or a friend, a former friend, wanted to borrow more money, and neglected to specify what sort of interest he would pay.

"Do people borrow money from you regularly?" Monica asked.

"Not *regularly*," Sheila said, laughing. "I'm not a bank, after all."

But, yes, there were friends, former friends, artist acquaintances, people from the old days, the early years, Morton had oscillated between helping them out ("He was enormously generous, it was a form of his contempt") and telling them to go to hell; and Sheila of course had inherited them.

"It isn't in my nature to say 'no,'" Sheila said. "But it makes me ill to keep on saying 'yes.'"

If Monica questioned her more closely, however, or offered to deal with one or another of these "friends" for

Sheila, Sheila abruptly changed the subject.

Was she restless, edgy, ill-tempered?—cursed with a perpetual headache? It had nothing to do with her work, she said defensively, or with her private life: it was just December: the approach of the solstice: the malaise of relentlessly darkening days and relentlessly lengthening nights. Too many gunmetal-gray skies boring a hole in the top of her skull.

Monica said, almost too brightly: "'There's a certain Slant of light,/ Winter Afternoons——/ That oppresses, like the Heft/ Of Cathedral Tunes——'"

"Yes," Sheila said, narrowing her eyes, wiping at her nose with the back of her hand, "—you've got it, friend."

Now she had time, a great deal of time, it seemed, to spend with Monica.

Time for sudden lunches in the village (at the tiny pretentious Soup du Jour, at the Glenkill Diner where workingmen ate) when Monica had barely an hour between classes, and was breathless, exhilarated, gratified (ah, she couldn't deny it!) to be seen about town, so companionably, and, as it were, *casually,* with Sheila Trask. They no longer met in the Academy faculty club, however, because Monica was rather jealous of her friend's attention: she didn't want her colleagues joining them, or overhearing their conversations and repeating them elsewhere. And Sheila liked to dress in old paint-splattered clothes much of the time. And she laughed loudly if something struck her as amusing. And of course Monica could never tell beforehand what sort of mood Sheila might be in.

Time weighed so . . . curiously on Sheila's hands now, she fell into the habit of telephoning Monica at odd hours. Just to say hello. Just to hear Monica's voice. (She was lonely, she confessed—"in fact greedy"—for a human voice.) Or she drove to New York City on business . . . but returned that very day, late at night. Her nerves were worn raw, she said, by the city: she simply couldn't take the excitement and she refused, she categorically refused, to tranquilize herself the way her friends did. Then again she planned to spend ten days in Puerto Rico with an old dear friend, but never managed to book a flight; she spoke vaguely but with a nagging persistence of taking Monica with her to Morocco, to Tangier, for six weeks. *That* was a place to see, Sheila claimed. And what people she knew there!—not the sort Monica spent her days with, at the Academy.

"Morocco?" Monica said. "Tangier?—of course I can't go, Sheila. My spring break is one week, not six."

Sheila didn't seem to hear. "If it's money you're worrying about," she said carelessly, "I'll take care of the plane tickets and expenses. All the expenses. In any case we'll be staying with friends of mine, not at a hotel. You'll love their villa on the water—it's primitive but beautiful."

"It isn't money," Monica said, hurt. "You must know it isn't money."

Sheila was bullying, Sheila was apprehensive. She fell into the habit of pacing about in Monica's company, restless, joking, telling long convoluted anecdotes, her monologues pitched high enough to be funny—often supremely funny —so that it was easy to overlook their underlying despair.

What is wrong? why wasn't she working? *wasn't* she working?

She never quite heard Monica's questions.

She would drop by at Monica's house with a surprise gift of food, gourmet food, from an Olcottsville store—a lovely caviar pie, a great hefty wedge of Stilton cheese, a French country pâté worth its weight in gold—and two bottles of Algerian wine (bought, as Sheila happily boasted, at a remarkable discount): ignoring Monica's smiling protestations that she had a great deal of work to prepare for the following day, and she hoped to get to bed early.

No matter, no matter: Sheila was lonely, Sheila was restless, Sheila was hilarious: in one of her exuberant moods.

She could be funny about virtually everything, even suicide—the subject, the theory. ("As Nietzsche says, the thought of suicide can get a person through many a long night—don't you agree?") She was certainly funny about men. ("If a man doesn't betray you it's probably because he *can't.*") She smoked, she fell into fits of coughing, she was clearly drinking too much, and very likely (so Monica guessed: she didn't dare ask) taking amphetamines. Her black eyes had acquired an unnatural glisten and her skin gave off a whitely radiant heat. Speaking, speaking rather too rapidly for Monica's taste, she ran her hands nervously through her hair, and gestured far too flamboyantly. It was tiring, Monica thought, simply to watch: she would have liked to take hold of Sheila's hands and make them still.

One of Sheila's new subjects was the phenomenon of aging.

A reverse miracle, she called it.

Yes it was banal and, yes, it was tragic—the tragedy being that it *was* banal.

At a certain age, Sheila said, trying to be amusing, mirror-selves—"mirror-ghouls"—begin to appear. "You discover that you really were vain all along," she said. "You were so supremely vain you never had to look—! But now you *do* look, more and more frequently. Because of course you can't anticipate what you'll see. How ravaged —that face of yours. How estranged. How *terrifying.*"

But Sheila didn't sound as if she were terrified, chatting away in Monica's presence, crossing and uncrossing her long legs, eating most of the food she had brought for

Monica; draining glass after glass of wine. Monica had the idea that Sheila had stopped eating at home—that she only ate in Monica's house, or seated across from Monica in a restaurant—and that the act of eating had become a queer little ritual to her: she ate quickly, greedily, yet in a way shamefully, as if she resented Monica watching, if Monica were not eating. ("Aren't you hungry?—have some of this," Sheila would say, and Monica would say, embarrassed, "Sheila, I've had dinner," and Sheila would say, as if not having heard, "This stuff is so fucking *expensive,* somebody has to eat it: come *on."*)

She spoke of getting older, always older.

The clock, she said, ran in one direction only: that was its subtle trick.

Her eyes were black, blackly moist, and the veins showed faintly blue at her temples: how strange she has become, Monica thought, staring: how beautiful!

She began to speak of her mother's death—and then stopped.

And Monica did not dare take her up on the subject, knowing, from past experience, that Sheila could not be interrogated.

". . . She too was terrified of it, the mirror-ghoul," Sheila said, raising her glass in a mock toast. "'I don't know who that woman is,' she'd tell us, '—I don't know who that *thing* is and I'm not going to look again.' But she knew, she knew."

Monica licked her lips and said softly that she was sorry.

"Sorry? Why?" Sheila said irritably. "The mirror-ghoul is waiting for you too—even if you are a golden girl."

Sheila disappeared, spent the day in Philadelphia, flew to Boston, flew to San Francisco . . . then suddenly she dropped by at Monica's without telephoning . . . or left scribbled notes stuck in Monica's door (her handwriting was virtually indecipherable, Monica spent long anxious minutes trying to read it: suppose the message were important?). She returned several times, nagging, insistent, to the subject of Morocco; six weeks in Morocco; a villa on the sea; and perhaps a visit to Egypt as well; had Monica ever been to Egypt? ("Of course not," Monica said, laughing, "—you know I haven't been anywhere." "Then we'll find you a Moslem lover," Sheila said zestfully, "—and maybe you'll never want to come back to Pennsylvania.")

Once Monica came home to find Sheila lounging in her station wagon, smoking a cigarette and examining Monica's mail. She had not torn open any of the envelopes—so far as Monica knew she had not slipped any in her pockets —but she behaved rather guiltily when Monica confronted her. "In case your husband, your former husband, is harassing you," Sheila said. "I thought I'd better check. I don't want you to be upset, Monica—you *know* you get easily upset."

One windy Sunday afternoon Sheila rode her chestnut gelding Parsifal ("Would any other name do?") across the fields from Edgemont, arriving disheveled and flushed at Monica's house; and, unfortunately, at a supremely awkward hour. Monica had student themes to correct, lessons to prepare, letters to write ("Really? letters? to whom?" Sheila asked suspiciously); and, though she hesitated to tell Sheila, she had a dinner engagement that evening with a man from town—one of the Academy's attorneys, to whom she had been introduced by Jill Starkie.

("This very nice man," Jill had said, "—this very, very nice, lonely, *civilized* man!—oh I know you will like him." And Monica did like him, to a degree.)

So she explained to her friend that she was busy; desperately busy; and Sheila was offended at once. "In fact

I'm rather busy too," Sheila said. "I only rode over on a whim since we haven't talked for a day or two. I just wondered how you *are*—I really don't intend to stay."

"Will you have a drink, at least?" Monica said guiltily.

Sheila paused, as if to punish Monica. Yes, she would have a cup of coffee, black. No: make that a glass of white wine—if Monica had any of the Algerian left.

She sat, she crossed her legs, lit a cigarette, brought up yet again, as if out of habit, the subject of Morocco, Tangier, a trip along the Nile—she and Morton had taken the river cruise once, early on in their marriage, it had been a profound experience, Monica would certainly enjoy it. After the pressure of Sheila's show was over *she* would need a change of scene, at least.

"That's true," Monica said uneasily. "But I can't join you."

Sheila stayed less than twenty minutes and had only a single glass of wine. She looked tired and confused; she looked her age. On her way out, zipping up her grimy quilted jacket, winding a blood-red mohair scarf around her neck (one of the few gifts of Monica's she had condescended to find a use for), she said, suddenly, that Monica should be aware of the fact that the Academy was exploiting her. Did she know? Or didn't she want to know? "The world is filled with people eager to drain your blood from you if you allow them," Sheila said mysteriously. "And you're the kind of woman, Monica—I saw this from the start—who isn't capable of protecting herself."

Monica managed a reply, half irritated, half amused.

She was quite capable of protecting herself, she said.

Sheila strode out to her horse, her handsome burnished Parsifal, she mounted him, too proud, or too indifferent, suddenly, to glance back at Monica. And Monica stood in the doorway, shivering, stubborn, refusing to call out good-bye. (Yet it would be no trouble, in fact it would be a

delight, to cancel her evening with Keith, to prepare a cas-
serole dinner for Sheila and herself, or some chili—Sheila
was inordinately fond of chili—and set her alarm for six in
the morning so she could finish her work then. It would be
no trouble, in fact it would be a delight. . . .)

She said nothing. She stood in the doorway, shivering,
watching, as soft wet clumps of snow fell, blossom-sized
clumps, in utter silence. Precisely when horse and rider
disappeared into the falling snow—along the lane, by the
edge of the woods—she could not have said.

In the women's lounge of the Olcottsville Inn, some hours
later, Monica dropped coins into a pay telephone and
dialed Sheila's number. Urgently she listened to the ringing
at the other end of the line—the ringing, ringing—in the
emptiness of Sheila's kitchen, in that long drafty living
room—in the glassed-in porch piled high with books and
old magazines—in the upstairs rooms (which Monica had
never seen)—and in the studio; ringing and ringing, defiantly unanswered. (If Sheila were in her studio, and
surely she was, the telephone would be disconnected. And
no one, no one, could connect with her.)

Monica hung up, received her dime back, tried again.
Perhaps she had dialed the wrong number out of nervousness.

Again, the ringing. A forlorn sound. Tinged just slightly
with anger.

The women's lounge of the Olcottsville Inn was in fact
the Ladies Lounge, fleshy-pink like the inside of a candy
box or a womb; ruffled organdy curtains, a deep-pile crimson carpet, the unromantic odor of disinfectant overlaid by
a perfumy air spray, lily of the valley perhaps. Two mirrors
framed in simulated antique gold reflected each other, and
a brass chandelier, endlessly—"Dear God it's the old Ver-

sailles effect," Sheila had once said, snorting in amusement, "right here at home!"

Monica listened, listened.

And still the telephone rang. And no one was going to answer.

When she returned at last to Keith (her "date" for the "evening": the vocabulary couldn't be denied) he would greet her with an air of gentlemanly warmth and expectation, a pleasant smile, no doubt he would rise from his chair as she approached the table, he *was* a gentleman, very nice as Jill had promised, very civilized, and quite clearly lonely; not the sort of man to feel, or to express, annoyance, that his "date" had been away so long, making a telephone call.

Fortunately they were not—"Keith" and "Monica"—at the stage where Keith might say, Are you worried about something, Monica? distracted? What are you thinking of, Monica, if not of me? us?

4

To whom was Monica writing, Sheila had asked.

Not meaning of course to be rude: for Sheila never meant to be rude.

(Sheila was a very poor correspondent, she confessed. Perhaps it had something to do with her temperamental inability to believe in the existence, the ontological existence, of people who were not immediately present, in the flesh; not, in a manner of speaking, in the room with her. "Then you forget very easily, do you," Monica had said lightly, and Sheila had replied, "Well—I try.")

But Monica made the effort, Monica certainly tried.

Romance is ephemeral, friendships can be permanent— so Monica came to understand, during the heady years of high school and college when she'd been, certainly it was pointless to deny it, an extremely *popular* girl . . . or, at the very least, an extremely *popular personality*. Even then Monica had seen that her friends, her girl friends, might well mean more to her in the future than her boy friends; and had not a thoughtful aunt warned her she would never have the opportunity to make such intense friendships again, once adolescence was past? So Monica wrote letters; dutifully, zealously, Monica wrote letters; though it hurt her unreasonably when one of her friends failed to respond to a second or even a third letter. . . . Harold had pretended to admire Monica for her faithfulness but in truth he'd thought her effort rather naive. *He* carried on no friendly correspondence at all; he simply hadn't the time; nor had he (if it came to that) the friends with whom to correspond.

"Women are different, I suppose," Monica had said doubtfully.

So she wrote her letters. By hand. Curled up on the sofa or propped up in bed, writing slowly, with deliberate slowness, hearing her own interior voice, imagining a one-way conversation: which is better, Monica thought, than no conversation at all.

Then it happened, to Monica's chagrin, that a letter she had mailed off to her friend Rebecca in Boston was returned—Rebecca had moved, no forwarding address—and Monica, disappointed, opened her own letter, and, reading it, was astonished at what she found: for was this voice, this smug little boastful voice, her own...? It was not simply that the Monica of the letter spoke with a false ebullient air of her work and the "amicability" of her divorce, but that she managed, not once but several times, to drop the name of Sheila Trask. And so casually, as if inadvertently. Sheila Trask the well-known painter.... Sheila Trask who is a neighbor.... Sheila Trask the widow of Morton Flaxman, famous for his ...

Sickened, Monica thrust the letter away; sat huddled, for a long time, her head in her arms.

Sheila Trask my neighbor, Sheila Trask my closest friend, Sheila Trask whom I see nearly every day and who is (or so it seems) wonderfully fond of *me*.

5

MONICA WAS LEARNING never to make inquiries, even sympathetic inquiries, about Sheila's work.

Monica was learning never to make inquiries at all.

"It isn't interesting," Sheila would say coldly, "—it's boring."

Or, fixing Monica with her razorish lopsided smile: "You don't *really* want to know, so let's change the subject."

Quite clearly something was wrong in Sheila's life—the pressure of the upcoming exhibit, perhaps—telephone calls, unexplained, that left her embittered and shaken—but, in the right mood, she was as irresistibly funny as ever. She told droll tales on herself, wildly comic episodes out of the past, or something that had occurred just the other day in New York City ("There was this man, actually he didn't look like a bum, on Houston Street, urinating a few yards from the sidewalk, absolutely no shyness, certainly no embarrassment"); she was drawn into laughing herself once it seemed that Monica, her uneasy audience of one, would laugh. Monica strained to see the logic of her friend's humor and fell after a few minutes into her mood —slapdash, wide-eyed, deadpan, *funny*.

Morton, Sheila said, had a very peculiar sense of humor: sometimes he laughed exuberantly, wonderfully; sometimes he merely stared in contempt. "I could never depend upon him," she said casually.

It was at about this time that Sheila, teasing and cajoling, finally persuaded Monica to join her on one of her pub crawls, as she called them, along the highway, over in Edgarsville and Swedesboro. There were, she claimed, "marvelous" places, never frequented by the genteel residents of Glenkill, bowling alleys, country taverns, dance halls, truckers' hangouts, that sort of thing, it was precisely what Monica needed, and what Sheila herself needed, as a change of pace. "You're actually becoming a stiff-backed little prig," Sheila said, "—'Miss Jensen' of the Glenkill Academy."

Monica winced, and laughed, as if the remark were just a joke; as of course it was.

Smiley's Place, County Line Tavern, Jake's Lanes & Barbecue, Hedy's Café, Swedesboro Inn, Mitch's Bar & Grill, Buddy's Circle Café, Black Billy's . . . Places where you never ran into anyone you knew, Sheila said, and never anyone who knew *you*.

So: in remarkably tight shiny-black trousers and a green satin shirt, Sheila was "Sherrill Ann," a lively divorcée from the Edgarsville area who worked for the telephone company, or was someone's secretary, or who owned a beauty parlor on a small scale; and Monica was a pretty blond named "Mary Beth," also a divorcée from Edgarsville, who wore a red turtleneck sweater, and blue jeans, and a locket on a thin gold chain, and who worked in the same office with Sherrill Ann, or was it in Sherrill Ann's beauty parlor . . . ? They appeared to be friendly, forthright, uncomplicated girls, good-natured girls who enjoyed draft beer and bowling and casual conversations, standing at the bar side by side with men, but always insisting, *always* insisting, upon paying for their drinks themselves; and by leaving together, as they'd come.

At this point in their lives, Sherrill Ann allowed it to be known, they didn't need male escorts no matter how well-intentioned and they didn't want male solicitude, they'd had enough, God knows, of that—five children between them: they were simply out to have a good time and to get home before their babysitter became impatient.

Which meant: they did not give out their telephone numbers, they did not even give out their last names, they weren't being coy and they certainly weren't playing games, and, yes, they paid for their own drinks. Every time.

Which meant: they were fun-loving girls who didn't take themselves too seriously.

Sherrill Ann in her satin blouses tucked in tight, her funky suede vests and hoop earrings and wide leather belts, Sherrill Ann in high-heeled kidskin boots, chain-smoking, laughing uproariously as she traded witticisms with the men; Sherrill Ann with a midsouthern accent (wasn't it?) but vague about her background, well you see she and her husband moved around a good deal, he was the restless kind, the kind who couldn't be trusted, as events subsequently proved. Mary Beth was the quiet one, Mary Beth was blond, and snub-nosed, and sweet, and blushed easily, while Sherrill Ann joked with the men, argued companionably about horses, Irish setters, farming, hunting and fishing, local politicians, cars, pickup trucks, tractors . . . which were good bargains and which were not. Sheila, high after two or three steins of draft beer, laughed without restraint at rather crude remarks—remarks Mary Beth pretended not to understand or didn't in fact understand—but Sherrill Ann wasn't the kind to take shit from anyone, should anyone get too forward.

(On their way home Monica wondered aloud, half in awe, half disapproving, how Sheila could bring herself to say such things, to strangers!—and Sheila explained that that was just the point, they *were* strangers; they didn't count. "Mary Beth takes things too seriously, in any case," she said.)

On these frantically comic evenings Sheila wore her hair brushed loose and crinkling on her shoulders, or pulled back tight in an old-fashioned ponytail—"one of the styles," as she told Monica, "of my lost innocence." Like a hatcheck girl she applied crimson gloss to her lips; she did something elaborate and fanciful with her eyes; her cheeks, normally so pale, were most beguilingly rouged. As to her perfume—well, it was powerful; it was *potent*. The luridly shiny material of her blouses grew taut against her small high breasts when she inhaled; the outline of her firm, similarly high buttocks was the more pronounced by her horsey stance at the bar. She knew her way around, did Sheila—that is, Sherrill Ann: her gaze low, level, mocking, flirtatious even as it was supremely indifferent.

Monica disliked the taste of draft beer, Monica disliked the smoke in the air, but, well, after one or two steins at the County Line Tavern, one or two at Buddy's Circle Café (where the hillbilly band Delaware Gap played weekend nights), after a nightcap at Flaherty's on the way home south on Highway 30 . . . well, she didn't quite care what she liked or disliked, it was all wonderful good fun, Sherrill Ann was indeed a "character," and Mary Beth was no slouch either, she was beginning to loosen up.

The men had names like Grady, Buzz, Billy, Orrin, Mason, Ryan. They worked at the Massey-Ferguson plant in Bethany, or at a General Motors plant in Edgarsville, or they drove trucks, or had small farms, or were auto mechanics, or were "between jobs." Most of them were married—to a degree. Unless they were divorced. They drank a good deal but they didn't invariably get drunk though sometimes of course they did get drunk but that didn't mean—didn't always mean—they would turn difficult or nasty or maudlin or hopeful. They were likely to ask Sherrill Ann and Mary Beth if they wanted another drink, or maybe supper somewhere, or, maybe, would they like to dance . . . ?

"Sure," said Sherrill Ann, wriggling her hips, "I'm game."

("How come you don't want to dance?" one of the men would ask Monica, and Monica would say, embarrassed, speaking quickly, "I don't know how to dance these dances," and the man would say, "Hell it's easy—I'll teach you," and Monica would say, "I'm afraid I just don't like to dance, I'm clumsy on my feet," and the man would say, smiling, baffled, sometimes glancing down at her feet, "You sure don't look like you'd be clumsy—c'mon and I'll show you." And Monica would say, no longer laughing, "Thank you, but I'd rather not," and the man would say, "Your friend's dancing, ain't she?—Jesus look at *her*," and Monica would say, sharply, to bring an end to it, "Yes but I'm not my friend, am I, I'm someone else.")

If the men were initially attracted by Mary Beth's wavy pale-golden hair and her reassuringly pretty face—the small upturned nose, the delicate features—they gradually came to prefer Sherrill Ann's presence, her queer excited exuberant manner. Mary Beth might have been as young as twenty-one, Sherrill Ann might have been as old as thirty-five, but it scarcely mattered because Sherrill Ann was the live one; Sherrill Ann was *hot*.

Monica who was Mary Beth, Mary Beth who was Monica . . . now a little drunk, borne along by a faint buzzing sensation in her head . . . but holding herself steady . . . perfectly in control . . . Monica who had done her eyes up cleverly too, black mascara and greeny-silver eyeshadow, Monica with her wavy hair, her watchful intense look . . . she *was* learning to loosen up, relax, have a good time. She wasn't a prig, surely, why just look at her: laughing at the jokes: humming with the music: sliding an arm around Sherrill Ann's waist as, laughing, swaying, Sherrill Ann slid an arm around hers.

She wasn't drunk but she laughed loudly, her hair falling in her face.

She wasn't drunk but it did strike her as funny—the seriousness with which men looked at her, and at Sherrill Ann in her satin blouse and bouncy ponytail.

It *was* funny . . . the fact that, years after his death, Elvis Presley was still king of the jukebox, with eight songs listed including one called "America" which Sherrill Ann professed to love. (Mary Beth's own favorite was "Huggin' You" by Billy Joe. There was also a rock-and-roll number by a band called Forced Entry, a guitar number by a band called Jump-in-the-Saddle, a breathy love ballad by the Pindee Sisters—all jukebox favorites.)

Funny too were the Christmas decorations at the Circle Café (blinking red and white lights, tinsel looped across the walls like festive cobwebs, green plastic trees above the bar, florid-faced Santas advertising Pabst, Schlitz, Miller High Life, Miller "Lite," Coors). Black Billy's had a near-life-sized plywood Santa's sleigh, complete with reindeer, nailed atilt on its sloping roof; Hedy's had frosted windows with red candles painted on the glass; tinsel was draped across the twelve bowling alleys at Walt's, just above the pins.

And here was Sherrill Ann dancing and cavorting like a girl of sixteen, Sherrill Ann clowning as she bowled (her freestyle technique, all legs and elbows, resulted in both gutter balls and spectacular strikes, to everyone's amusement), Sherrill Ann mock-serious about a game of pool, a white camellia pinned drooping to her hair. She prided herself on keeping pace with Grady and Ben and Buzz and Orrin, matching them drink for drink—or almost. She argued the finer points of horse breeding with them, she commiserated with their angry tales of "unfair" alimony and child support payments, the custody rights they had to live with. The courts—the lawyers—the welfare workers —were all biased against men, against men who were fathers but ex-husbands: that was a fact of life! that couldn't

be denied! It's just what they can suck out of you, Grady,
or was it Buzz, complained to Sherrill Ann,—after they
decide they don't want you no more; and Sherrill Ann,
feeling subdued that evening, said, People shouldn't get
married, maybe, in the first place, "—Hell, just look at
me."

One night Monica found herself watching Sheila intently, by way of a fly-specked mirror behind the bar of the
Swedesboro Inn, thinking, What is she doing? and *why?*
Sheila was dancing with a trucker named Mick, or Mike, a
former state trooper (why former, no one knew), her left
arm slung across his shoulder and her right arm crooked
tight at the elbow, the man's arm—beefy, thick, covered in
dark hairs—pressed hard against the small of her back.
The music was drawling, throbbing, standard country-and-
western from the jukebox; the air was stale with smoke; the
dancers were both slightly high, their cheeks touching,
their bellies, their thighs. Their feet scarcely moved.
Watching them, idly, yet intently, her eyes burning from
the smoke in the air, Monica told herself that she wasn't
embarrassed for her friend, or annoyed: Sheila was only
joking, pretending, behaving like a teenaged girl with her
first boy friend . . . or like a teenaged slut. Monica saw the
man sway suddenly, as if he were about to fall; she saw
Sheila grip him hard to hold him upright; she heard
Sheila's strident laughter. The man then kissed her, or
made an attempt, half-clowning, yet surely seriously, and
Sheila eluded him; she simply pushed him away. It was all
good fun. It was all *fun*. Wasn't Sherrill Ann after all
wearing a "suede" cowboy hat that evening, slanted rakishly across her forehead, and very tight boy's jeans—
which she claimed to have found somewhere at Edgemont,
left behind by a forgotten guest?

She returned to Monica, she interrupted the man who
had been talking to Monica (about the insult of his salary

check being garnished, for alimony payments, by order of the Swedesboro County Court), she said laughing: "Okay, Mary Beth, knock it off—you two lovin' it up here—our babysitter's going to give us hell if we don't get our asses out of here *now*."

Sometimes on their way Sheila talked Monica into stopping impulsively for a pizza (a "freak pizza" with *all* the works), sometimes for a stack of pecan waffles topped with whipped cream, or the Strawberry-and-Almond Baghdad Surprise, at the International House of Pancakes—though Monica could do no more than take a few bites, and Sheila rarely got through half of what she ordered. It was the *idea*, after all. It was the *atmosphere* of the pizzeria, and the pancake house.

All innocent, Monica thought. And fun.

If a little crude.

. . . But innocent, surely. And so different from her real life (her life as a teacher, her life, her ceaseless dinning life, in her head), surely it was healthy and rejuvenating and good for the soul, as Sheila claimed. ("I suppose we're too narrow, too cautious," Sheila brooded. "We *could* pick up a couple of men and bring them back to my place . . . or stop at a motel . . . what do you think? Do you think it would be worth it? Or would it just be *trouble?* and *boring?*" Without waiting for Monica's reply she said, as if thinking aloud: "Hell, they'd just give us the clap, or knock out a few teeth. The fun of it now is what we do— and what we don't do.")

Sometimes when Monica was insufficiently Mary Beth— not sufficiently mollified by drink, that is—she had to admit that the excursions were exhausting, and beginning to be predictable. The tobacco smoke made her slightly ill, the noise from the jukebox made her head ring, there were indefinable odors she hated, and there was, inevitably, and

frequently, the women's lavatory. . . . The jostling in the
barroom, the crowding, the loud good-natured bantering;
the bantering that turned into bullying; the outright propo-
sitions, delivered in a tone of "fun" (Let's go somewhere
and fuck right now, men might say to Sheila, and Sheila
would say, simply, Nope); the rivalrous women who might
have been wives out for a good time, an illicit good time,
or divorcées, or semiprofessional hookers—the women
who eyed Sherrill Ann and Mary Beth with both shrewd-
ness and resentment. And poor Sherrill Ann sometimes
drank too much, trying to keep up with the boys, and got
sick to her stomach in one or another filthy lavatory or
parking lot . . . or at the roadside, on their way home.
(Monica generally drove, on Sheila's bad nights.) Once
Sheila gripped her arm—squeezed it—said in an elated
voice, "You're a good sport, Mary Beth, hon,—*I wouldn't
have predicted.*"

And Monica felt, despite herself, an immediate flood of
childish gratification.

What of Sheila and *men,* Monica wondered. What did she
really think, what did she really feel, about *men . . . ?*

It was hard to take them seriously, Sheila said. Then
added, with a sly narrowing of her eyes: "It's hard to take
anyone seriously."

If Monica tried to draw her out, to make inquiries,
Sheila seemed rather aloof; or, perhaps, shy; everything
was deflected into a jest, an airy bon mot, a shrug of her
thin shoulders. When she was slightly drunk she boasted of
herself as a woman who liked men and who sometimes
craved men but, in fact, she could "take them or leave
them: it's all so banal in the end."

Except for Morton, of course.

Except for Morton whom she had—well, hadn't she?—
loved.

"Been crazy about, you might say,—'crazy' about," Sheila said, rubbing her hands over her eyes. "But that was a long time ago, Monica."

Evidently there were no men in her life at the present time except friends—artist friends—two or three "gentlemen farmers" in the area—acquaintances and connections in New York, Key West, Mexico, North Africa. And Paris. Sheila showed Monica the photograph of a Jamaican Parisian, as she called him—a muscular, near-bald black man, very handsome, very sure of himself, who, dressed in a paint-splattered sweater and jeans, bared his magnificent teeth at the camera. What do you think of Henri, Sheila asked Monica, nudging her as a man might nudge another man, contemplating the photograph of a sexually attractive woman, and Monica said, smiling, wondering if she were *meant* to smile, "Well—he's certainly unusual. Was he a lover of yours? Is he, still—?"

But Sheila only grunted; laughed rather contemptuously; and took back the photograph. "Thus, *Henri—!*" she said.

When Sherrill Ann and Mary Beth went out for one of their evenings on the town, it was Sheila's task, undertaken with zest, to fend off men if they grew importunate or bullying, or overly affectionate. At Jake's, or Hedy's, or The Place, or Walt's Bowling Emporium, Sheila liked to declare that they came unescorted and they intended to leave unescorted—and that was that.

As for Bud, and Billy, and Mack, and Mike—Sheila liked them so long as the conversation was amusing, the banter impersonal and breezy. She took offense, however, if one of them tried to interrogate her ("How many kids?— I thought you said three"), or if it appeared that sweet little Mary Beth was being made uncomfortable. In turn, she angered the men by muddling their names, or mixing them up ("Buzz?—oh yeah *Bud*—sure as hell you *are* Bud"), as if it scarcely mattered who was who. In the morning she frequently telephoned Monica to ask "how her head felt" and to sift through their little adventure of the night before, and it was clear then that she couldn't distinguish one man from another—Fitch, Grady, Max—Johnny, Steve, Jeb O., Ryan. She felt sorry for them, she said. Their jobs, their marital problems, their debts; their old-fashioned swaggering machismo with nowhere to stick it.

"If you feel such contempt for them," Monica said one morning, irritated because her head ached, and she knew she was doomed to drag herself through the day, "—why do you go out? Why do *we* go out?"

"I don't feel contempt for them at all," Sheila said. She seemed quite startled by Monica's remark; even a little hurt. ". . . I *like* them and I like it that they like me."

Monica carried the image of one or another of the men, the nameless men, around with her, at school, in her classroom, in the faculty dining room; she recalled the silly powerful downbeat of the jukebox; her sense—wholly irrational, wholly irresistible—that she was someone not quite herself, a girl, a golden girl, again, with all of her adult life ahead.

What she and Sheila did was chaste enough, wasn't it? —and innocent. And it was certainly exhilarating. To be looked at by strangers, and admired; to arouse some hearty male desire, however anonymous and futile; to know that she seemed—though assuredly she was not—mysterious. All of my life ahead, Monica thought, her lips curling in irony. She knew it was supremely foolish yet it *was* exhilarating.

(She had told herself at the breakup of her marriage that she had not been hurt, not deeply hurt, it wasn't that important, it wasn't that significant, her divorce like her marriage was "ordinary," "average," a "typical" sort of suffering: Don't take yourself too seriously, Monica! Of course Harold's sexual interest in her had gradually de-clined over the years. The nine years of their "relation-ship." It had begun with ferocity, a high keen rather pitiless passion, romantic if one chose to think it so, and flattering as well, for who, being fiercely desired, does not feel flattered . . . ? There was a day, however, more precisely a night, when Harold no longer looked at *her*, no longer re-quired looking at *her*, though he continued to require a body—a legitimate female body—to make his sexual per-formance "normal." Whether *Monica* and *body* were joined was a question, a tricky little question, fraught with embar-rassment, which she didn't dare ask. For there were no words. No words not thumbed-over, banal, stale. Monica could not reproach her husband after all when he betrayed her with her own body, making love—what "love" there remained to be "made"—to the flesh with which he shared a bed and a last name, while thinking, dreaming, plunging deep in his private thoughts. Perhaps, Monica thought, one of the phantom-inmates with whom he betrayed her was an earlier, younger Monica, mysterious and elusive, not yet *his . . . ?*)

But the exhilaration too was winding down.

Indeed, it was becoming too "exhilarating."

. . . Friday night at Buddy's Circle Café and there was great amusement at: Mary Beth's panic when a hard-shelled beetle fell (from the ceiling?) into her hair; Mary Beth's plight when, her bladder swollen from beer, she had to go to the women's lavatory but the women's lavatory (a single squalid room, a single toilet) was in use, in use, in use, in *use* . . . and, finally, under Buddy's protection, with Sherrill Ann also standing guard, she used the toilet in the men's room. ("Absolutely filthy," Monica said afterward, stung with humiliation, "—sickening," and Sheila said, laughing, indifferent, *"I've* been in worse and was grateful enough at the time—you're just spoiled.") A Thursday night at Walt's Bowling Emporium outside Swedesboro, much noise, gaiety, gaiety that seemed in fact sheerly noise, and there was Sherrill Ann the divorcée and mother of two (or was it three) strutting about, clowning, in a new shiny-leather jumpsuit (funky overlarge zippers, trousers pegged at the ankles), drawing the attention of men she and Mary Beth had never met before, drawing their attention rather too successfully, so that, before long, there was an unpleasant exchange—which hadn't any air of romance about it, or intrigue, or simple interest—"cock-teasing bitches," they were called, "dykes who ought to have their heads knocked together," they were dismissed as, finally: which Sherrill Ann professed to find amusing.

("Don't you think it might be dangerous," Monica said, "—now that they're coming to know us." "They don't know 'us' at all," Sheila said curtly. "That's the point: no one knows 'us' at all.")

And then it happened, one night later in December . . . a tavern outside Edgarsville, a carload of men, Sheila and Monica were hurrying across the parking lot to Sheila's car when one of the men called out to them, his name was Fitch, Fitch'd taken a liking to Sherrill Ann a few weekends ago, but there was some beef between them, the reasons weren't clear, maybe he was mistaking her for another woman but he didn't think so, Fitch was anxious for them both to get in his car, Fitch was saying that Sherrill Ann had promised to meet his kids, hadn't she said she wanted to meet them, he'd shown her some snapshots and she'd said she wanted to meet them, now she pretended she didn't know who the hell he was, what the hell did she and her girl friend think they were pulling . . .? Fitch's friends followed after him, they were all a little drunk, good-natured drunk, maybe not so good-natured if Sherrill Ann wouldn't cooperate, if Mary Beth kept dodging away like they were lepers or something, like they were shit, Fitch was saying that Sherrill Ann and him, they had an understanding, and now she pretended she didn't know him, "We got some talking to do," Fitch said, "honey you promised, you know you did," and Sherrill Ann told him to please leave them alone, they were on their way home, they were late getting home, their babysitter would call the police if they didn't get home in the next fifteen minutes, and Fitch just said, "You two come along now, hon, we got some talking to do," and Sherrill Ann told Mary Beth to get in the car and lock the door, which she did, and Fitch tried to stop Sherrill Ann from getting in the car, "I don't like no bitch lying to me, I don't stand for no bitch lying to me," Fitch said, and Sherrill Ann said he was drunk, and they weren't getting in his car, and they *were* going home, and that was that. "Our babysitter will call the police," Sherrill Ann said, her voice raised, angry, perhaps just perceptibly trembling, "—she knows when we're expected home and she knows we've been *here*."

So the men let them go.

But followed after them in their car: tires screeching in the gravel, horn blaring, a terrifying twelve-mile run ahead from Edgarsville to the village of Glenkill: Sheila, white-faced, forced to drive at speeds varying from forty miles an hour to eighty-five, in her desperation to escape: and Monica, Monica limp with the conviction they would both die, hunched beside her, quietly sobbing, whispering, Why oh why why the hell, *why*. . . . Fitch was too drunk to drive so one of his buddies drove, pulling up alongside Sheila, edging toward Sheila as if to force her car off the road, roaring ahead, threatening to cut in front of her, while Fitch leaned out the window of the passenger's seat, shouting obscenities, gesticulating, a raised third finger jabbed into the air, a clenched fist shaken, at several points the two cars were so close that Fitch very nearly smashed Sheila's window,

flailing at it with his fist, all drunken high spirits, all in
good fun, just teasing the girls, just joking around, but the
girls *were* cock-teasers themselves they *were* asking for it
one of these days they were going to get it they hadn't
better show their faces in Edgarsville again. . . .

The chase ended at the Glenkill village limits; the men
dropped back; Sheila sped ahead.

At Monica's house Sheila said, putting her hand on
Monica's arm, "Look—we're all right and we weren't in
any real danger but if you're upset, I mean if you're really
upset, I can stay the night here, or"—and here her voice
wavered, here, she sounded frightened, herself, "you could
come home with me, I feel responsible for this, I feel like
hell."

Yes, Monica thought, in anger, you should feel responsible: *you—!*"

Aloud she told Sheila that she was really all right; she
was grateful to be alive; she only wanted the evening to
come to an end.

"You're not angry. . .?" Sheila said.

"I'm too exhausted to be angry," Monica said, opening
her door, wanting only to be alone, gone, away from
Sheila.

6

SHEILA SAID CARELESSLY that suicide, in her family, wasn't all that "significant" an act.

"The thought is—when you've had quite enough you've had *quite* enough," she told Monica.

She had fallen by degrees into the habit of telephoning Monica every evening around seven, when Monica was certain to be back from school. (Unless of course she was out for the evening: which Sheila would want to know.) Just to say hello, just to see how Monica was. As for herself, why things were going well, things were going as well as one might expect, perhaps it was best not to inquire.... Sometimes, unlocking the door of her house, Monica heard the telephone ringing and felt an immediate pang of dread; of apprehension. She was exhausted from her day at the school and she was exhausted by the thoughts that spun about in her head and she was exhausted, exhausted by... But she couldn't not answer the phone: Sheila might know: Sheila might understand.

Perhaps because she wasn't working very steadily now —Monica gathered that was the case—Sheila had become unnaturally sensitive to nuances of meanings, to slights. If she asked Monica politely whether Monica was too tired to speak at the moment, her pose was misleading, for Monica didn't dare admit to being tired, on the contrary Monica was obliged to assure Sheila that she wasn't at all tired, not at all: in fact she was delighted to hear from her since she had intended to call Sheila herself, in another ten minutes.

"Are you certain?" Sheila asked doubtfully. "I can call back another time. I can call back tomorrow."

"Not at all," Monica said, "—let's talk *now*," leaning her forehead against the cold metal of one of the cupboard doors, closing her eyes, feeling an old headache resume. It was almost comforting, that old dull ache.

Sheila was in zestful high spirits, Sheila was moody, depressed, "down." She'd heard from a friend but it was bad news; or, perhaps, good news—with the promise of changing her life. ("But only after I get my exhibit hung," she said mysteriously.) How was her work going?—well, how was *Monica's* work going? (This said with an air of innocent malice.) Most of the time she fended off Monica's concern with a flippant reply but occasionally she said, flatly, quietly, that things were not moving along as she had hoped, not at all as she had hoped, in the early morning, before dawn, she lay in bed paralyzed with dread at getting up and going across to her studio and beginning another morning. "Still, suicide requires magnanimity of spirit, don't you think?" she said. She extended her hands— stretched out her fingers—contemplated them—glanced at Monica.

"*I* don't think I'm capable of 'magnanimity of spirit,' do you, dear little Mary Beth?"

"I can't answer that," Monica said, suddenly helpless. "I don't really know you that well."

"Oh, as to 'knowing'—!" Sheila said. "I think we all 'know' one another only too well."

"Sheila Ann" and "Mary Beth" were never resumed; as if by mutual consent, the names weren't mentioned for some time after the Edgarsville incident. Then, abruptly, Sheila began to make allusions to the highway, the "pub crawling," and how lonely Sherrill Ann was going to be without Mary Beth. . . .

Monica stared at her, and asked what she meant. Surely, after their narrow escape, Sheila didn't want to go back?

"We wouldn't return to Edgarsville, of course," Sheila said. "There are plenty of other places. . . . Look: nothing like that would ever happen again. I can guarantee it."

Monica said ironically, "I can guarantee it too."

Sheila laughed; allowed the subject to drop; but, from time to time, resumed it, as if to needle Monica. She hinted that "Mary Beth" was overly timid and puritanical; and had become, of late, obsessively concerned about her professional image.

Monica said stiffly that she didn't feel obliged to defend herself.

Sheila said that there was no need for her to defend herself—she wasn't being attacked.

Monica said she'd lost her taste for country taverns, for bowling, for draft beer—the very smell of it would nauseate her—and, in any case, she'd only gone to keep Sheila company, to accommodate Sheila, there never had been any "Mary Beth" at all.

Speaking quickly, rather defiantly, Monica broke off in embarrassment, while Sheila regarded her with bright, black, amused eyes. ". . . There never was any 'Mary Beth' at all, you say?" she murmured. "Oh but I don't quite believe *that:* you've just packed her away somewhere."

Sheila didn't ask Monica to accompany her again, though, from time to time—always casually—she alluded to being "lonely," and to finding it "even a bit of a bore"—Sherrill Ann without her pal. But Monica, forewarned, refused to be drawn out. She had had all that, she thought, with a thrill of elation—*that* was behind her.

7

SHE CAN HEAR the telephone ringing as she unlocks the door, ringing, ringing, that forlorn reproachful note, sounding through the empty house. Keith murmurs something to the effect that he hopes—given the lateness of the hour: midnight—it isn't bad news and Monica doesn't trouble to reply, she feels her heart beating slow and hard and resolute, no her fingers are not shaking, no she is *not* even annoyed, when, snatching up the receiver, saying hello, repeating hello, hello, yes, hello? she discovers that there is no one on the line: that her caller has (perhaps) simply dialed her number, laid the receiver down, walked away, forgotten the entire transaction.

Lately Sheila has been calling at odd, wayward hours.

In all fairness it might be said she doesn't know the hour: she has been working round the clock in her studio; and/or, she has been drinking.

"I hope it isn't anything . . . ?" Keith says. A tactful man, a gentleman, he keeps his distance; stands in the doorway; allows Monica her privacy.

Monica says, "It's a wrong number. It's nothing."

She breaks the connection; dials Sheila Trask's number; discovers that the line is busy, indeed the line *is* busy, the receiver is off the hook at Edgemont as she had suspected. . . .

"Nothing," says Monica lightly. "A prank."

Next morning, early, before seven, Monica telephones Sheila.

The receiver is raised at once, on the first ring, but Sheila explains—swiftly, rather coldly—that she can't talk at the moment: there has been a minor household emergency: poor Siegmund was out all night and now he's sick, vomiting, very likely someone poisoned him, one of Morton's old enemies in the neighborhood, she'll have to drive him to the vet's.

"I'll call you later," she tells Monica, then, about to hang up, adds, "I hope it wasn't anything *crucial—?*"

8

"ARIADNE'S THREAD HAS snapped, and now the poor creature is wandering in the labyrinth," Sheila said, yawning and stretching. "But she'll emerge. One day soon. She always has in the past. —Otherwise she'll starve, she'll suffocate, to hell with her."

"If there's anything I can do . . ." Monica said hesitantly.

Sheila laughed. Then she said, soberly: "You're so kind, Monica. But thank you, no, I don't believe there is anything you can do. Just *be*."

Sheila was in one of her ecstatic high-flying moods, Sheila was in one of her dull-eyed stupefied moods, exhausted, grainy-skinned, not very attractive. She spent her mornings driving about on country roads, she spent her mornings on the telephone, suddenly there was a houseguest at Edgemont (a relative? a cousin of Sheila's?), suddenly she turned up at Monica's, carrying a bag of groceries, goat's-milk cheese and Norwegian rye crackers, that very same country pâté she loved to gorge on, and two six-packs of imported German beer. God she was hungry!—famished!

Another thing too: the way the days passed, spun, a sun and a moon and a sun again, zip and it's through: you get to the point where you sit hypnotized by the clock, any fucking clock, watching the hands move, forgetting to breathe.

Did Monica understand?

And there were the mirror-ghouls, the mirror-leeches.

"Sisters" of a sort. Whom you don't recognize though they seem to recognize you.

Did Monica understand?

Or was it simply subterfuge, like "Mary Beth"?

Monica had been planning to spend the week after Christmas in Indiana, visiting her family; but now she worried about leaving Sheila alone.

Not that Sheila wanted to celebrate Christmas with her, or to exchange presents: she detested Christmas, she said, and she detested ceremonial presents.

She detested the very time of the year . . . the taste of the air, the texture of the light. The old, old eclipse of the soul. . . .

At her age, Sheila said grimly, cheerily, the seasons spin and you don't need to be reminded of the "new" year, or forced to realize that it's the "old" come round again.

Happy holidays! Safe drinkers make safe drivers!

Still, she suspected that Monica was the kind of person who innocently thrives on holidays. A secret talent for the domestic, for mulled cider, roast turkey with oyster dressing, emotional bric-a-brac, no? yes? "What of your friend Keith?" Sheila asked carefully.

"What of him?" Monica said.

"What are his plans for Christmas? Is he staying here, or going away?"

Monica tried to think.

"I don't know," she said finally. "Maybe he hasn't any."

Sheila stared hard at her, smiling, critical. "This is the time of year," she said, "when everyone has plans. Except —those who don't."

"*I* don't have any plans," Monica said.

Sheila lit a cigarette; yawned again, and stretched, luxuriant as a cat; deliberately spoke of other matters . . . every chimney, every bloody chimney, at Edgemont needed repairs . . . and vandals, neighborhood kids, were driving their snowmobiles through her fences, tearing up her fields . . . and the sable brushes she'd been using since the age of fourteen seemed to be deteriorating in quality in direct proportion to their increase in price. As to Siegmund—the poor dog *had* been poisoned, Sheila was convinced, though the vet was too cowardly to say so, he wouldn't have wanted Sheila to go to the police and drag him into it. Poor Siegmund!—it was a mercy when he was finally put to sleep but mercy hadn't come quick enough, he'd certainly suffered.

Monica's eyes stung with tears. "I'm sorry to hear that," she said. "I was very fond of Siegmund."

"Well," said Sheila, sucking on her cigarette, frowning as if the taste repulsed her, "—Siegmund was very fond of you."

Monica invited Sheila and Keith to dinner, so that, at last, they might meet; but though Keith accepted the invitation readily, happily—he *is* lonely, Monica thought—Sheila made polite vague excuses. She had already met the man, she believed. That is, they'd been introduced, years ago, Keith Renwick wasn't it?—she had no clear memory of *him* but she remembered the name.

Monica felt unreasonably hurt, irritated.

Sheila said, as if to mollify her friend's response: "I'm only comfortable with lawyers when they're in my pay."

As if to counter Monica's invitation, Sheila telephoned her a few days later to invite *her* for cocktails at Edgemont —to meet the sculptor Jake Halleron— "of whom I'm sure you've heard: his work is everywhere"—an old friend, an old friendly rival, of Morton's. Halleron turned out to be as striking in his way as Morton Flaxman had been in his: very tall, six feet five or so; with cadaverous cheeks, sunken eyes, a fringe of metallic-gray hair about a gleaming bald pate; long arms, long legs, long blunt-fingered hands and unusually large square nails. He was courtly,

flirtatious, leering, yet amiable; well-spoken; given to odd
little malicious side-glances at his hostess, as if they shared
a good deal—a common past of which it would be indis-
creet to speak; given too to a British sort of whimsy, overlaid with sarcasm. He lived in Venice, did he?—no,
Monica misunderstood: *Vence.* But he had a residence, a
studio, in Montauk also—Montauk, Long Island, perhaps
Monica knew the area?—he was living there with his mé-
nage, or was it a *menagerie*—the witticisms, the innuendos, came fast, sly, slurred, and were gone by the time
Monica thought to smile. She felt intimidated by him, and
wondered if perhaps that was the reason for Sheila's invitation.

An older man, very nearly an old man, in his late six-
ties, perhaps, Halleron behaved in a most youthful manner.
He wore a pale red silk shirt with white embroidered trim
and a white string tie, a Western costume, clearly a costume, but Monica could not make out if it was meant to
amuse, on this snowy Sunday afternoon in Pennsylvania,
or to impress. Sheila had shampooed her hair, and looked
quite the country squire's wife—tweed skirt that fell to
midcalf, black-knit stockings, an oatmeal-colored cash-
mere sweater Monica had never seen before, a red scarf
tied at her neck. Her manner with Halleron was provoca-
tive; combative; yet oddly deferential; for of course, as
Monica thought, he was of Morton Flaxman's generation
—it was not absurd to imagine him and Sheila as lovers.

Sheila made an attempt, rather strained, Monica
thought, to draw her into the conversation; to interest Halleron in her—in *her* as a professional woman, a woman of
intelligence and taste; but clearly the focus of interest, the
excited focus of interest, was Sheila Trask and Jake Halleron, their common—but surely not commonplace—past;
the people (living, dead, moribund, "vanished") they
knew; the works of art, seriocomic or tragic adventures,

anecdotal episodes, they shared. Scattered on the coffee table before them was a pile of snapshots Halleron had brought, through which they had been sorting before Monica's arrival; earlier in the day Sheila had shown Halleron her new paintings and was now basking, or smarting, in the aftermath of his response. Which accounted in part for her bright, brittle, nervous, yet elated mood; her air of girlish coquetry; the shrill sound of her laughter and the sudden, abrupt, melancholy cast of her expression. Her glances at Monica—moist, darkly bright, shadowed—were indecipherable, and quite disturbing.

Are they lovers, Monica thought, suddenly frightened, —have they been lovers?

Then, more calmly: It has nothing to do with me, in any case.

The visit lasted no more than an hour yet would be one of those queer undefined experiences—pockets, or vacuums, of experience—common to any life: inexplicable, unsettling because inexplicable, but too troubling to be dismissed. During the course of the hour Sheila drank a great deal but seemed rather more in control than she had been, of late; Halleron could have little idea of the stress she was enduring, the wild fluctuations of mood and temper. Their talk surprised Monica by being so relentlessly specific, even gossipy—they talked not of art but of artists and galleries (Halleron was a mine of droll little anecdotes, some of them quite nasty, all of them amusing: he forbade either Sheila or Monica to repeat a disturbing tale of the last days of Philip Guston, told to *him* in strictest confidence); and, in regard to Sheila's work, exclusively of technique, "references" and "allusions" and "tricks" of which Halleron seemed generally to approve. Where Monica had seen beauty of a kind, indefinable, haunting, evanescent, where Monica had supposed she saw meaning, Halleron spoke of a canvas with a visible weave; a diluted pigment soaked into the canvas; staining, puddling, rubbing, blotting, brushing; the use of a turpentine spread; washes; areas of dried paint and "false space"—the influence (elegiac, yet perhaps rather too emphatic) of Hans Hofmann; and one or two other tricks, gimmicks, which, in his opinion, Sheila hadn't quite mastered. And the hand—the heavy hand!—of Flaxman: that was still a factor, distracting to him, though not perhaps to anyone else.

He glanced at Monica, and winked.

As if inviting her to corroborate his remarks?—or to contradict?

Sheila listened, listened hard, baring her teeth in a small smile to show that she wasn't taking Halleron's words *too* seriously—she wasn't hurt, or upset, or confused, or angry—that simply wasn't Sheila Trask's style.

In any case, Halleron said, more kindly, Sheila had interesting problems to solve.

"Yes," Sheila said in a subdued voice, staring at the glass in her hand, —"I suppose you could say so."

When Monica rose to leave Sheila said she should stay for dinner if she liked, but Sheila's manner was distracted, her invitation not very convincing or persuasive. Saying good night, with Halleron in close attendance, Sheila made an impulsive, uncharacteristic gesture: she brushed Monica's cheek with her cold lips in a hostess's perfunctory farewell, and squeezed her fingers with the promise of telephoning soon.

Monica felt the imprint of that ghostly kiss, that cold improvised farewell, and wondered at its significance, all the way home.

Though perhaps it had no significance, apart from the fact that Halleron had been close by, observing.

9

NO CALL CAME; but Sheila herself dropped by, uninvited, without giving Monica a warning, clearly high—alcohol, pills?—the strain of Halleron's visit?—the following evening.

She brought a six-pack of beer, she seemed rudely unaware of Monica's concern (for Monica had work to do: truly, Monica had a good deal of work to do), she sat on Monica's sofa and talked, chattered, yawned, joked, complained wistfully and bitterly and with a wild despairing humor, for an hour—for an hour and a half—while Monica made an effort to calm her, to puzzle out what was wrong. This visit, impromptu and not entirely desired, reminded Monica uncomfortably of Sheila's very first visit to the house—that surprise visit—it seemed so long ago, now—years ago—when Monica had been too confused to know whether she liked Sheila Trask, felt a powerful attraction to her, or was, in fact, repulsed by her. So brash! —so loud!—so self-absorbed, even as she expressed the most damning sort of judgment against herself, as if challenging Monica to agree.

Yes, she was drunk. And though Monica had no choice but to "like" her now—they had gone too far for that—she wished the woman gone for the evening—for the night. For the remainder of the year.

Sheila did not resemble a country squire's wife now. Her hair was uncombed, she'd thrown on a dirty sweatshirt and manure-stained jeans, for, clearly, it little mattered in Monica's house what she looked like; nor did it matter what sorts of wayward, bizarre, pointless things she said. No need for pretense, *here*. She spoke bitterly of enemies —detractors—hers and Morton's—gallery owners who had cheated them—"friends" who were misleading Sheila even now—the world of art parasites—reviewers, critics, promoters, dealers, collectors, "art historians"—all parasites, yet highly regarded—richly rewarded—admired, pursued, sucked-up-to. God, how she detested them!— wished them all dead!

She finished one can of beer, opened another, tossed the ring-pull on Monica's coffee table. Monica asked about Halleron—was he married, was he still working—but Sheila seemed scarcely to hear. She said: "But what am I speaking of except—mortality. Always and forever *mortality*. Nothing else engages me, nothing else terrifies me, but I can't seem to translate it into work, my mind is racing, spinning, it's going around in circles and I can't get off, every syllable I utter is the sheerest self-pity and I'm not imagining it—my brushes *are* lousy. Fucking bloody lousy my very *brushes*, it's no wonder I can't work, have you ever heard anything more pathetic—?"

Of course the woman was funny, deftly funny, her facial mannerisms, her gesturings, her verbal timing—all very skillful indeed. But Monica refused to laugh. Monica stared at her, unsmiling, and said: "Sheila, please. Don't. Don't go on like that. If I can do anything to help, I will, but . . ."

Sheila regarded Monica with a look of affectionate contempt. Deliberately she sucked at her beer, wiped her mouth, rose to her feet with an air of precarious dignity. "'But,' says Mary Beth quietly, 'But,' says sweet little Mary Beth, meaning 'Get out of my house,' meaning '*I* can't be the one to put you out of your misery, or to comfort you, you'll have to hire a professional for *that*, my friend.'" She set down the beer can, snatched up her quilted jacket, prepared to leave. "I shouldn't have come over. I'm simply presuming upon your good nature. Your too-good too-sweet blond nature. Good night!"

Monica followed Sheila into the kitchen, protesting. She didn't want Sheila to leave, she said. Why didn't Sheila stay for another drink, or for dinner...? Why didn't she tell Monica what was wrong...?

"It's the holiday season," Sheila said cheerfully. "None of us is responsible for what she says or does. Or thinks."

"But what *is* wrong, Sheila?" Monica asked. "Why can't you work? Why are you so unhappy? You seem so changed—"

"I never change, I simply become more myself," Sheila said, making a comical face, a little-boy face, as she zipped up her jacket, wound her mohair scarf around her neck. Her attention was drawn to her reflection—hers and Monica's—in one of the kitchen windows; she pulled Monica more closely beside her, so that the two of them faced the window. "...One a death's-head, the one *so* blond. It must be the genes, the cheekbones. The soul poking out through the skin. Or *is* the soul skin? Everything on the surface, everything in two precise dimensions, as it should be. Good night, and Merry Christmas!"

Monica, suddenly alarmed, stricken, followed Sheila out onto the porch. The wind blew raw stinging bits of snow into her face. She tried to take hold of Sheila—tried to grab her hand but the woman's thin strong fingers slipped through hers. Sheila said sharply: "I don't care to be patronized, Monica. Above all I don't care to be *touched.*"

Monica watched her drive away, thinking, frightened: I'll never see her again. Something terrible is going to happen.

And again, and again: I should have forced her to stay. I should have embraced her. What did she mean, *to put her out of her misery, to give comfort . . .*

10

THE TELEPHONE RINGS but it is never Sheila.

Now, suddenly, it is never Sheila Trask: and Monica does not dare telephone her.

She receives an invitation to dinner from Brian Farley's wife; an invitation to dinner from Jill Starkie ("On Christmas Eve, Monica, if you're going to be *alone*"); Keith telephones with flattering frequency; there are even a few wrong numbers, just to rouse her, to send her pulses racing. She will fly out to Indiana after all—there is no reason not to go—she misses her family or in any case the idea of her family, a family, a *home*.

On December 24 she spends much of the day trying fruitlessly to get into contact with Sheila.

Dialing the number again and again, listening to the ringing at the other end, her mouth hard with resentment. She tastes something sour—sour and metallic—she stares at the featureless sky, a gray corrugated landscape. It is the winter solstice, such misery, but now the sky must yield to light, to warmth, to the new year, to life; or so the legends promise.

When at last Sheila Trask lifts the receiver Monica will say quietly: "I hate you, why *don't* you die," but, fortunately, Sheila Trask never lifts the receiver. Perhaps in fact she is already dead.

On Christmas morning Monica drives to Edgemont, as she had vowed she would *not*.

She notes that Sheila's station wagon is parked in front of the carriage house, lightly dusted with a powdery film of snow. There are no other cars around.

She climbs the stairs to the studio—her footsteps loud, clattering—she wants Sheila to know that she is here—*she* is here—and she is damned angry.

She calls out: "Sheila?—it's Monica. Let me in."

She raps at the door. Tries the handle.

"Sheila? Are you there? I know you're there—let me in."

The door is locked, no one answers. Monica had a single glass of bourbon to fortify herself before driving over and it seems to her the bourbon *did* do some good, her nerves are tingling with excitement, with exhilaration, her voice does not shake, she is very much in control.

"Sheila? Please—it's Monica."

She tries the doorknob again.

She stands panting, head bent, listening, to the floorboards creaking a few yards away. Sheila? Sheila, listening intently to *her?* She can see the woman's white, tense, cunning face . . . the sickly radiance of her soul . . . those dark eyes flashing with malice, with spite, triumph. . . . Monica hates her, yes, truly, Monica Jensen hates Sheila Trask, but they have gone too far for that, it is too late for that, she wishes her dead, yes, but she is faint with terror that perhaps the woman *is* dead and she has come too late to help.

"Sheila *please*," she says softly, now leaning her head against the door, "—God damn you, *please*."

She can sense that Sheila has come to stand close by; on the other side of the door. A foot away. Less than a foot away. On tiptoe, in stealth, in spite and triumph, Sheila, her nerves taut as Monica's, her skin as burning, eyes narrowed. No she will not unlock the door. Yes she will—she *must*.

But no. Evidently it is to be no.

She presses her warm face against the door, close, very

close, to Monica's, her skin is a dull sickly white, Monica can feel the heat of her body, its secret trembling. Monica says softly: "Sheila—I know you're there. I want you to unlock this door. Do you hear? I want proof that you're all right. Then I'll go away again—I promise. But I want proof, God damn you, that you're all right—that you haven't hurt yourself—you aren't sick. Do you hear?"

She hears the woman's breathing—ah, unmistakably!—quick, hard, hot, panting. An animal's cunning, an animal's panic. That rank fleshy smell.

When she turns the doorknob she can feel Sheila's grip—Sheila's resistance.

Monica drops her voice, says in a honeysweet drawl: "You, Sherrill Ann, I *know* you're there, so come *on*. Sherrill Ann? Hon? This is Mary Beth—you *know* who this is."

But the ploy is awkward, unconvincing; embarrassing.

Monica will henceforth hate Sheila all the more, for having brought her to such shame.

Her head is pounding, her eyes smart with tears. She is furious. She considers the panels of the old door—the solid oak door—and wonders what strength it would require, what anguish her fists would have to absorb, if she managed to smash it in.

She says, surprised at the calmness of her voice: "Sheila. Do you know the date?—Christmas? I only want proof that you're all right, I just want to *see* you, and then I promise I'll go away."

But Sheila will not, will *not* reply.

And what humiliation, for Monica to be so exposed!—she, Monica, who has guarded herself so closely!

"Tell me to leave, then. Tell me to go to hell. As long as I know you're all right, you aren't sick . . . haven't injured yourself. . . ."

She senses a movement behind the door, inches away.

She hears Sheila draw breath to speak.

But there is no response.

Nothing.

So Monica says quietly: "I'll leave. I think I can assume that you *are* all right—you can take care of yourself." She pauses; steps back. "I won't trouble you any longer, Sheila. Do you know, I'm sick to death of this, of you, of everything—I'm sorry we ever met—I don't really know *why* we met. I never intrude where I'm not wanted so I'll leave now, and please don't contact me again."

Her voice quavers with triumph, and with a delicious malice of her own. She knows she has won; and now it is a matter simply of leaving, descending the stairs with dignity, with grace, yet quickly enough, before she loses her advantage.

If I fall, if I hurt myself, *she* is to blame—*she'll* regret it, Monica thinks. Her head aches violently and her cheeks are wet with tears though she hasn't been aware of herself crying. But she reaches the bottom of the stairs without incident. And no one calls her back. And she can hear no sound at all except her breath—hoarse and raw—and the pounding of her blood.

Absurd, absurd, such pounding—!

"You'll regret it," she whispers.

PART III

"Holiday"

1

GOING HOME FOR a week would be a restful experience, Monica thought. A kind of convalescence, in secret.

A curative strategy, to go where no one knew her.

Of course she had to cancel several social engagements in Glenkill, and, for courtesy's sake, she had to sound greatly aggrieved at doing so. She *was* aggrieved—these days, she carried grief into all the corners of her life—and it was no difficult matter to make people think that her regret had something to do with them.

In any case, she did not want to give offense.

She did not want to fail, here.

She was remembering, these past few weeks, why it had seemed so important to her—so crucial to her well-being, her very life—to be "liked" as an adolescent, to be "well-liked," indeed to be "*very* well-liked." It was all very American, all quite innocent, this early faith in popularity. A ring of smiling admiring faces was a powerful solace for private hurt, and even if one was liked for much that one was not, still the attention was gratifying. Monica recalled how, as a girl of fifteen, secretly unhappy—secretly miserable, in fact—she had been buoyed along by the fact that other girls in her class envied her.

Yet Keith Renwick's interest in her felt oppressive; a sort of sham. She did not deserve it, she did not want it, yet it *was* gratifying, and probably harmless. He was a bachelor who had been, as he so fastidiously phrased it, "involved" with a woman for several years, so romance was, for him, as awkward as it was for Monica. (She had told him very little about her marriage and divorce—she was in the habit now of alluding to her past as merely typical, statistical, of no great personal significance.)

Love was a category of being, as was friendship. But the prefatory stage of a relationship was undefined—the prefatory stage of their relationship, at least. If she and Keith were sleeping together, Monica thought, she could say to herself, I have a lover, and it would appear to mean something. I have a lover now. I have a lover *again*. But they were not sleeping together and they were not in love and so far as Monica knew they were not friends.

"When you come back from Indiana, will you telephone me?" Keith asked; and Monica said, with that false warm enthusiasm that so characterized her these days, "Of *course.*"

Monica had already mailed Christmas presents home—she was guiltily punctual about such matters as holidays and anniversaries—but at the last minute she drove to Philadelphia to shop for more. A giddy little drunken little shopping spree. She had not done anything quite like this in a decade. Where does the money come from, she asked herself gaily, using her credit card, pulling bills out of her wallet,—have I become suddenly wealthy? Her holiday had begun. At last. Perhaps she would regret it later, in January, when the bills came due, but that was later, that would be the "New Year."

In Indiana, in Wrightsville, in the Jensens' spacious old brick-and-stucco house on Arlington Boulevard, there was a good deal of hugging and kissing and exclamations of surprised delight. How pretty Monica was!—how good, to see her again! The strain of confronting everyone after so long—nearly two years—was eased by the semihysteria of the holiday season. If Monica began crying suddenly no one took special notice; or, if so, her agitation was believed to have something to do with the holiday season and with the long rocky plane trip from Philadelphia.

Monica was to enjoy herself in Wrightsville, Monica was to relax, to look alertly about and to take her cues from other people. A time of suspension, a time of protracted innocence. In Wrightsville she had always been "Monica Jensen," a daughter and a granddaughter, a sister, a niece, a cousin, long before she had become "Monica Bell" and disappeared somewhere in the East. This was the only place in the world where Monica had never *not* been "Monica Jensen," which was comforting. Here, she was a young girl, still, newly confirmed in the Anglican faith. A daughter cherished by both her mother and her father. A very good student despite the fact that she was so extremely pretty, and often extremely careless about school. She took piano lessons each Saturday morning at ten o'clock from a plump perspiring woman of late middle age named Mrs. Martin who wore shiny dresses, ropes of pearls, and large button earrings, and who liked nothing better than to take Monica's place on the piano stool and demonstrate, with zest, how her lesson should sound: "Now pay attention!—I will *not* repeat." At school Monica had girl friends and boy friends, always a girl friend who was her "closest" friend and a boy friend who was her "steady," though the identities of these girls and boys changed over fairly brief periods of time. Now, if she could recall a name she had no idea of its place in the sequence of years that constituted her school "life."

Still, Wrightsville was the place of golden years, the place of small petty heart-stopping triumphs.

How pretty Monica is!—they said, eyeing her closely.

How wonderful to see Monica again, when was the last time she was here?—ran the voices.

The handsome gift Monica had originally bought for Sheila Trask was received with much enthusiasm by Monica's sister-in-law. ("Why, this is beautiful, Monica," Esther said softly, drawing the turquoise Peruvian shawl out of its wrapping, "—wherever did you find anything so beautiful," she said, as if sensing the shawl's high worth and the unlikelihood that it was truly meant for her.)

In all, the second wave of Monica's presents went over well. Though there may have been some bewilderment among her family about why, so very suddenly, she had grown lavish, bountiful, nervously eager to please.

How happy how very *happy* she was to be home, and how very happy they were to see her: except, on the second day, Monica's mother ventured the opinion that she looked "just a little tired," "a little pale," and wondered if perhaps she was working too hard; and Monica said, hurt, annoyed, that she wasn't at all tired, she was feeling exceptionally well, she was so happy to be home how could she possibly look tired!

"Only about the eyes, dear," Monica's mother said.

A six-day visit, and five days to go.

A sweaty disagreeable sleep, a body pressed upon hers, the sensation in her loins as sharply acute as if a man were entering her—penetrating her—an erect penis jamming itself into her body.

But they were not in Monica's girlhood room, in her bed, they were (suddenly) dancing: grinding their bodies against each other: trying to kiss with bared teeth.

Angry. Greedy.

And what shame: for people were watching, it was in a public place, a ring of strangers formed to stare.

Monica woke and the sensation in her loins vanished at once.

She could have wept, she wanted it to remain; wanted it to flower into something yet more keen, more powerful.

Her heart was racing unpleasantly, a trickle of perspiration ran down her side. No, she didn't want sexual excitation, she didn't want even to think of it, not now. She didn't want the memory of her husband or of any other man, defiling her now.

You see I *am* happy here, Monica thought, in this place where you have never been, and where no one knows your name.

She made her way like a sleepwalker through her old life, through the rooms of her old life, hardly daring to breathe, feeling her heart go faint with . . . was it love? . . . surely it *was* love . . . love for her parents, and a sense of precariousness, doom. Her father's face was deeply creased, he had aged visibly since Monica last saw him; she supposed she was partly responsible. (The breakup of Monica's marriage, the surprise of her divorce, the mystery of her "current situation," the problem of her "future." How had it happened, Monica's father demanded, that she was teaching in a preparatory school in Glenkill, Pennsylvania?— *why* had it happened? Why didn't she receive alimony payments from Harold? And if it was a teaching career Monica wanted, surely she could teach elsewhere, in Indiana, perhaps, in Indianapolis, why not here in Wrightsville where she needn't live alone . . . ?) Several years ago Monica's mother had been hospitalized with a severe bladder infection, from which she had never entirely recovered. At the time of the diagnosis Monica had thought at once: Cancer. She had thought: Now we will all be punished. But it wasn't cancer, Monica's mother had not died. (Because she hadn't died, however, Monica was obsessed with the idea that something in the universe was wrong, their good fortune was undeserved, she herself was indebted to God, in whom she had been incapable of believing since the age of fourteen . . . which fact even now endangered her mother's life. Confessing this curious reasoning to Sheila, Monica had wondered if, in her soul, she was still a child; still infantile in her expectations. Sheila had said, Of course, aren't we all . . . ?)

Six days at home, in the old house on Arlington Boulevard, overlooking the Lutheran cemetery. Six days' grace. She pleased her mother by working with her in the kitchen and by eating heartily at meals; she pleased her father by being pretty, vivacious, uncomplicated, as he remembered her. Why, she even played some of her old piano pieces for them, out of her battered *Piano Classics* book—a Mozart minuet, several short preludes of Chopin, Schumann's "Träumerei"—the long-forgotten notes leaping, it seemed, out of her very fingertips. She played haltingly, stiffly, yet she did remember the pieces, it was remarkable how she *did* remember, while she had forgotten so much else.

Shortly before Monica boarded her plane at the Indianapolis airport her mother embraced her impulsively, and rather hard; leaned back to stare at her; and said in a lowered voice that she was holding up well—far better than she would have done, under the circumstances. "You're a strong woman," Mrs. Jensen said, regarding her critically, "—though you don't look it."

Monica laughed, though she felt obscurely insulted. "Why should it mean that much?" she said carelessly, stepping away from her mother. "It was only a friendship, after all."

2

AND IT *HAD* ended, simply and irrevocably; it had burnt itself out. And that was that.

Amen, Monica thought.

She was free to make other friends—free to *not* make other friends—to do whatever she wished.

In Wrightsville she'd gone with her sister-in-law Esther to get her hair cut and blown dry in a style that lifted airily from her forehead and made her eyes look larger, more exotic. In Wrightsville, sequestered away in her old room, she had spent several intoxicating—and exhausting— hours poring through scrapbooks she'd kept in high school, seeking out Monica the golden girl, Monica the prom queen (her junior year: had that been the dizzying height of her social life?), so that she might take heart from these early successes. She had known how to smile, then, as these snapshots suggested—she had known how to express happiness even if she hadn't always felt it. So, thought Monica, inspired, I will try again: I will *be* that girl.

To a degree, that is. For, after all, she would be thirty years old in a few months.

She postponed telephoning Keith Renwick as she'd promised. Then, one day, seeing him walking along Main Street of Olcottsville with a woman—an attractive young woman in a fur coat, wearing oversized stylish glasses—she reasoned that perhaps there was no longer any purpose in telephoning.

If he wants to talk with me, he will, Monica thought. If not, not.

Still, she felt the ignoble pang of mimetic desire: wanting someone hitherto unwanted, because, or so it appears, that person is wanted by another party.

And isn't there always something ignoble about desire, Monica thought. Mimetic—or otherwise.

Sheila Trask's watercolor, in its bamboo frame, set inside a beige matting: the delicate little painting Sheila had claimed to be unable now to "see."

That work of art . . . which Monica halfway wanted to return to the artist (so her spiteful pride urged her); but which, in calmer moments, she knew she must keep. Returning it to Sheila would mean its immediate—unsentimental—destruction. And though she no longer had any feeling for Sheila Trask (she *didn't* hate the woman—not at all) she felt a curious attraction for the watercolor itself.

She stood before it, studying it. A remarkable technique, watercolor: it has to be executed so swiftly, in a matter of minutes, with a very few felicitous strokes of a brush: no margin for error, for second thoughts, for blotting out and beginning again. In this case the artist captured (ah, "captured"!—how Sheila would scorn such jargon) a winter scene—early winter—pale earth colors mixed with the slightly soiled cast of the snow—trees that were of no distinctive beauty, and nearly leafless—outcroppings of rock—the ruins of an old stone building, perhaps a barn: and all that was mysterious about the painting, all that it *was,* seemed to have virtually nothing to do with its object, and only to do with the intensity of feeling in the artist; in the eye and the hand that had so skillfully "captured" the scene, the mood, that passing moment. So Monica stared. So Monica brooded. It was a pity, she finally decided, that she had never known the woman who had painted the watercolor—she had only known the Sheila

Trask of the present, who not only detested such calendar art, as she called it, but was incapable of seeing it.

Now, art must be filtered through "mind"—whatever that means—and contaminated by it.

One Saturday in January, after the exhausting start of the new semester, it happened that Jill Starkie and her ten-year-old daughter dropped unexpectedly by Monica's house; Jill was driving her daughter home from ballet class in Olcottsville, and couldn't resist, as she said, paying an impromptu—"unpremeditated"—visit. She hoped Monica didn't mind: "I always dread interrupting anyone as busy as you," Jill said with a happy sort of apprehension, her eyes darting rapidly about as if to gather evidence of Monica's especial busyness. "But Molly and I will only stay a *min-ute*. We *promise*. Won't we, Molly?"

Monica smiled, smiled hard, and assured mother and daughter that they were very much welcome. Would they come inside, take off their coats, have something warm to drink? . . . it was so bitterly cold outside.

Within minutes sharp-eyed Jill had caught sight of the watercolor on the mantel.

"How beautiful—how exquisitely beautiful," she said, standing before it, clasping her beringed hands together, "—so very like a Chinese landscape, yet, you know, so unmistakably *American*. It's the ruins of the old poor farm, isn't it? Just a few miles away? The artist must be local," Jill said, squinting at the painting, "but I don't recognize the style. Isn't there any signature?"

Monica said, "I bought it in Olcottsville, I don't think there *is* any signature."

"Oh but surely there is, on the reverse?"

"No."

"Have you checked?"

"Yes—of course I've checked."

Something in Monica's voice prompted Jill to glance at her, still smiling, ecstatic with the surprise of the painting, not wanting, it seemed, the moment to end. "The artist *must* be local because the scene is only a few miles away —do you know, I hate to confess it, but I tried to paint those ruins myself, I tried and tried!—because it's so poignant, so devastating, I mean the look of it. I've seen lithographs of the poor farm, it was built in the early 1800s and modeled after a famous English mental hospital, I've forgotten the name, I mean the construction of it—the architecture. So ugly!—massive—yet in its way noble—I *can't* explain. But this watercolor captures it all—captures so *much*. And yet, you know, the implication is always— as it is here—it's always—with real artists—as if no one *tried*. As if it just—happened!" Jill said with a despairing sort of gaiety. "Which marks the artist and sets him apart from people like us: for we must try. And try and *try*. . . ."

"I bought it quite cheaply," Monica said. "They said they'd had it for years."

"But art doesn't age," said Jill, frowning, "—whoever are these people?—they sound so ignorant! Which gallery did you get it in?—or was it an antique shop?"

Monica murmured that she really didn't know; she'd forgotten.

"I wish I'd seen it first," Jill said. Then, hearing her own words, she added, guiltily: "Of course, the point is, I didn't—and you *did*."

Yes, Monica murmured.

Molly was clearly restless, so, sighing, Jill set down her mug of coffee and prepared to leave. She hoped that Monica would drop by to visit *her* soon—*any* time. She and James had been so very sorry Monica hadn't been able to come to dinner on Christmas Eve—but they quite understood—it was such a busy time of year.

In the doorway, winding her wool scarf around her

head, Jill returned suddenly to the subject of the water-color. The land along the Poor Farm Road was left unculti-vated, she said, because the Flaxmans owned it—that is, Sheila Trask owned it. "Everyone else around here rents out land for farming, but *she* can't be troubled, you know," Jill said, looking searchingly at Monica. "She's so ab-sorbed in her work, evidently, she can't take time to think about such pragmatic things . . . financial arrangements . . . like the rest of us. Isn't she fortunate? And so gifted. . . ."

"Is she?" Monica said.

After the Starkies left Monica moved the watercolor from her living room upstairs, to her bedroom. A smaller space suited it better, clearly. And now it would not be so need-lessly exposed.

3

SHEILA TRASK WAS, or was not, waiting for Monica to telephone.

But it made no difference in Monica's life, in either case.

She had her own life now, she had her own life, fully, again—her classes, in which she was deeply absorbed; her faculty and committee meetings; luncheons with colleagues, or with newly made acquaintances in town; a dinner party now and then; even an ambitious study-discussion group, informally organized by the younger members of the Glenkill school, that met on alternate Thursday evenings to take up the interpretation of "controversial" new ideas (deconstructionist literary theory, radical French feminism, the ethics of nuclear armament/disarmament, the knotty subtleties of the "biological revolution," American foreign policy in Latin America, and so forth: they were nothing if not happily eclectic). Monica went to chamber music concerts in the area, where she forced herself to listen, to listen hard, and not merely to hear, or to sit and allow her thoughts to wander where they would—in directions melancholy or otherwise; one bright sunny day she drove to Philadelphia to visit the art museum, alone—and ended up feeling rather too much alone, *too* emptied of all affect, in its eerie Duchamp wing amidst the iconoclastic images of an era long dead and never, for Monica, sufficiently alive. ("What am I supposed to feel?—*am* I supposed to feel?" Monica wondered, staring at that totally perplexing work of art, *The Bride Stripped Bare by Her Bachelors, Even (Large Glass)*, 1915–1923. The positioning of the finely cracked glass in the room suggested its mysterious worth—its sacred talismanic value—inaccessible, no doubt, to profane eyes. It was of little aid for Monica to read, in dutiful schoolgirl manner, that, in its perfect balancing of "rational and non-rational elements," the *Large Glass* ranked as one of the great works of the twentieth century; nor to be cryptically informed, by Duchamp himself, in a quotation affixed to the wall—"There is no solution because there is no problem.")

Returning from Philadelphia Monica drove some miles out of her way, to pass Black Billy's Tavern on Highway 29: a tawdry little place by day, hardly worth a second glance. In contempt she saw that a half-dozen cars were parked in the lot, nosed up close to the building; and it was only midafternoon. For the first time she noticed that Black Billy's was windowless—or, rather, the old windows had been paneled over, covered in what appeared to be aluminum foil.

But it wasn't worth a second glance, really. Or a second thought.

Monica also: prescribed for herself a swimming regimen, half an hour at the Olcottsville YWCA on alternate days, in the late afternoon or the very early morning; prescribed for herself a reading/research regimen, in connection with the books of classic American literature she was teaching in her advanced English classes—*The Scarlet Letter, Walden, Uncle Tom's Cabin, Leaves of Grass, Huckleberry Finn.* Of her own accord she initiated a Friday afternoon student reading hour, at which student writers read, with varying degrees of spirit, their own fiction, poetry, and journal notes. It was all very rewarding, very . . . exhausting. But very rewarding.

I can't talk at the moment, Monica would tell Sheila Trask politely when Sheila telephoned.

Thank you for calling, I'd been wondering how you were, Monica would say carefully,—but I can't talk at the moment, perhaps I can call you back tomorrow. Will you be home?

Out of curiosity, however, sheerly out of curiosity, Monica telephoned Sheila's gallery in Manhattan—the Laurence James Gallery, Fifty-seventh Street—to inquire about the upcoming Trask show. She had been reading about it, she said, vaguely, wasn't it scheduled for sometime in February?

No, the receptionist told her: the show was scheduled for late April.

"I thought it was February," Monica repeated.

It *had* been February, yes, but now it was rescheduled for April—April 27 was the opening. If Monica would like to leave her name and address, the gallery would be happy to send her an announcement.

Monica asked why the show had been rescheduled and was told, after a moment's pause, that the artist was out of the country.

"Out of the country! . . . she wouldn't," Monica said.

You can't manipulate me, Monica thought. God damn you.

By accident, a few days later, Monica learned that Sheila Trask had gone to Morocco after all, for one reason or another. Painting?—friends?—vacation?

As Betty Connor chattily explained in the A & P, where she and Monica had met, it wasn't that unusual for Sheila Trask suddenly to "pick up and go" at a minute's notice: and usually to somewhere exotic: she and Flaxman both. New Guinea, Kenya, Zimbabwe, South Africa—once to Afghanistan, Betty thought (hadn't it been written up in the local paper?—Morton Flaxman had come down with hepatitis). During Flaxman's last years it was generally known that he'd grown rather odd, eccentric, there was invariably an entourage of sorts that accompanied him on his trips, and camped out at Edgemont; "colorful" personalities; artists or would-be artists themselves. So far as Betty knew, however, Sheila Trask had gone off to Morocco by herself, and had told her housekeeper she wouldn't be back for a very long time—possibly not until the fall.

"The fall!" Monica said softly. "But doesn't she have a show this spring? . . . in New York?"

"Does she?" Betty Connor said, looking at Monica. "I really wouldn't know."

"A major exhibition, I'd thought. . . ."

Judging from Betty Connor's tone she knew nothing of the connection between Sheila Trask and Monica, and Monica felt both relieved and obscurely angered; but rather more relieved; so it was important for her to keep her questions casual.

"Yes," she said, "a major exhibition, or so I'd been told. . . ."

"Well," said Betty Connor, easing past, "I wouldn't know, I've never moved in that woman's circle."

Monica pushed her grocery cart on, Monica's head throbbed, it was unfair, it was malicious, without informing her, without saying good-bye, it *was* unfair—unjust; yet of course what one might have expected; supremely Sheila Trask; supremely selfish.

"I never intrude where I'm not wanted," Monica whispered.

As the minutes passed, however, she began to feel chilled; even clammy. Beneath her clothes she was perspiring but the dampness was cold. Like the onset of the flu— the worst strain of flu—intestinal flu—a malaise that slowly enveloped the entire body and sickened even the mind. She would have to leave, she was getting seriously sick.

Only with enormous effort did she continue. Shopping: pushing a grocery cart along the aisles of a food store: going through the routines of a life, *her* life: reaching with numbed fingers for familiar shapes—cans and bottles and gaily colored packages, items related in some utterly obscure and mysterious way to her well-being. These shapes, these brand names, these *things:* might they not be seen as calming, reassuring?—a confirmation of the fact that Monica knew very well who she was and what her tasks were and how most efficiently to execute them?

In the end she did not get sick in the A & P. The attack of nausea and faintness came later, when she was safely home.

4

ONE EVENING IN early February, in Keith's company, Monica found herself noting, with little emotion, that the textures of the world had subtly altered. What should have been shimmering, iridescent, mysterious, was now merely —surface.

An attractive surface, surely.

But surface nonetheless: two dimensions.

They were in the atrium dining room of the new Hyatt Regency in Olcottsville, a well-groomed well-mannered clearly well-suited young, or youngish, couple. In a setting of waterfalls; banks of poinsettias—red, pinkish-red, creamy-white; "appointments" of the most tasteful and unobtrusive sort. A pianist in a tuxedo, also unobtrusive, was playing romantic songs—"Smoke Gets in Your Eyes," for instance—so softly as barely to interfere with the splash of fountains and the hum of conversations.

Monica was having a martini, which she quite liked; she was listening to Keith speak knowledgeably of current political and financial and legal and moral crises, which he saw as "mutually interrelated." (The word *crisis* was a favorite of his, as was the word *impasse*.) Keith's irony was so gentlemanly, so carefully modulated, Monica could not always determine its significance. Did Keith detest the present administration in Washington, or was it the administration's critics he detested?

At one point during the lengthy dinner Monica heard herself say wittily, though perhaps not entirely appropriately, "Maybe there is no solution because there is no problem," and Keith regarded her with a quizzical smile.

Keith Renwick, a lawyer trained at the University of Virginia: tight-curled graying hair, warm moist intelligent brown eyes, a habit of nodding just perceptibly as he spoke: not explicitly aggressive but very much, one could tell, his own man. Monica liked him when she was apart from him rather more than she liked him when they were together, but perhaps that would be no problem—she'd felt the same way with Harold, early in their relationship.

After a long while Keith said: "There is always a solution—if you know whom to contact."

They were not lovers and there was some doubt as to whether they might ever be lovers—which of them would take the risk, make the irrevocable irremediable gesture?— and even friendship was doubtful, friendship was *quite* doubtful, but they were companionable together; they were an attractive couple, together.

And Keith was capable of surprising Monica, too: she hadn't the right to feel complacent about *him*.

For, as it turned out, Keith was extremely interested in survival—in survivalism. The survival of a nuclear holocaust, the breakdown of American civilization, that sort of thing.

Monica, knowing little about the movement, was surprised to discover a considerable library in Keith's apartment, magazines and handbooks—*Survival News, Best about Backpacking, Live off the Land, You and Yours, Rifles & Handguns Guidebook, Survive!* When she questioned Keith he was evasive at first, then spoke with mounting enthusiasm and authority. Of course, he said, he didn't take the paramilitary aspect of the movement too seriously ("Paramilitary?" Monica asked), nor did he make it a fetish to go camping, hiking, backpacking, under hardship circumstances, except for a few weeks each summer. Still, he said, seeing Monica's look of startled interest, no one can deny that the United States is extremely vulnerable to nuclear attack; and that, contrary to the most pessimistic theories, a good percentage of citizens *could* survive. "Of course these citizens would have to know how to go about it," Keith said, smiling faintly. "It won't be an amateur's world, postholocaust."

Monica leafed through a hardcover book titled *Life after Doomsday*. She noted lists of "primary," "secondary," and "tertiary" target areas in the United States: "anticipated fallout zones": "relatively fallout-free 'refuge' zones" (the Florida Everglades, the uplands of North Carolina, the Sangre de Cristo Mountains of New Mexico, the sand counties of Wisconsin) where survivalists could flock.

She said, with less equanimity than she intended, "Most of us would carry our own fallout zones with us," and Keith, as if prepared for that remark—as if, indeed, he and his brethren heard it all too often—replied, taking the book out of Monica's fingers, "Most of *you*—but not all of *us*."

5

MIDWINTER. LATE WINTER. Snow-stubbled fields and days of bright harsh slanted sunshine alternating with days when the sun never appeared—never emerged at all. Monica was sick for a while but others were sicker, it was the annual flu, a prolonged feverish malaise, passed desultorily from person to person, among the teaching staff, the students. Monica could not reasonably object to being sick if it meant that happiness was never a possibility, hence never an issue.

She wrote on the blackboard in her classroom, in a large clear hand: *Nature is hard to be overcome, but she must be overcome.* And what could Henry David Thoreau, so generally misunderstood as an uncritical nature lover, have meant by that enigmatic statement . . . ?

(He loves Nature, the brightest boys argued, but he hates *human* nature. No: he really hates Nature, beneath all the poetry. Or: he means something different from what his words seem to say.)

With a passion that might have had a good deal to do with her fevered nerves Monica threw herself into her classroom teaching; there was indeed the dizzying sense of falling . . . plunging . . . and surfacing again, greatly exhausted, at the end of the day. She did not become infatuated with her students, not even with the two or three most appealing boys, but there were certainly hours when she was so mesmerized by her own voice and her imagined image in their eyes, she felt the pangs of love; an almost carnal love; the not-wanting to break away, the not-wanting for the experience ever to end.

But of course it ended, invariably. The hours were only fifty minutes long and the weeks consisted of six days.

One day Monica received a letter from Harold and opened it swiftly, carelessly. She found no threats—no accusations—no sly troubling innuendos—only a dozen or so neatly typed lines inquiring after Monica's health and general well-being and supplying Monica with news of Harold's health and general well-being. And his professional "prospects." The letter was so perfunctory, so totally lacking in voice, Monica could not understand why it had been written. To assert that Harold still existed? To prick her into feeling jealousy? It seemed incredible that this was the person who had hired a private detective to investigate her only a few months ago. . . . By the graying opalescent light of mid-February that seemed wholly unlikely; but, by that light, nothing seemed likely.

Just let it go, Monica thought.

It happened that Monica, Miss Jensen, became a confidante of sorts for several boys (Mitchell, Alan, Jeremy, occasionally Sean) who were mysteriously unhappy because of problems at home. ("Ah, 'problems at home!'" Jill Starkie exclaimed with a sigh. "There are always, *always* 'problems at home.'") She was required to listen attentively and sympathetically; to proffer advice, in a judicious manner; to avoid cruel generalizations ("Adolescence is invariably a difficult time") since her students were individuals, defiantly and helplessly individuals, and rather proud of their plight. From time to time a boy actually wept in the privacy of Monica's office but she resisted the almost kinetic urge to touch, let alone embrace, fold in her arms, for *that* was not to be done, *that* would be folly indeed. Hadn't coarse-minded Sheila Trask suggested, a long time ago, that Monica's students might harbor erotic fantasies of her? And how much more ignoble, if Monica, deranged by loneliness, were to begin to harbor fantasies of them. . . .

The subject of survivalism was never again mentioned by Keith Renwick; nor did Monica wish to bring it up.

Nor did they speak at any length about their past histories. Surely Keith was curious about Monica's failed marriage but his manner was circumspect and tactful. He was too carefully trained in the law to wish to pose questions of a personal nature outright.

It was understood generally that each had been disappointed in love, each was more or less unhappy, if not mildly depressed, at the present time. Otherwise—what had they in common?

Monica calculated Keith's age as between thirty-seven and forty-three. (She afterward learned it was thirty-five.) His sandy graying hair, though receding from his forehead, grew thick and springy at the crown of his head; his nose was strong, full, wide-tipped; his eyes intelligent and watchful. He spoke with the faintest of midsouthern accents yet he laughed heartily, even zestfully, if the situation required. He played squash, tennis, and golf; he rose every morning at six without fail and swam two miles in the pool at the Olcottsville Athletic Club; he might have been a few pounds overweight, about the waist in particular, but he carried it well. A man of moderate height, with a moderate frame. And handsome enough, Monica supposed. A subject in two dimensions, a matter of affable surfaces; handsome enough.

If he felt sexual desire for her the desire was evidently well under control. In fact, it seemed to Monica that he treated her rather like a convalescent. (Perhaps Jill Starkie in her mildly hysterical way had hinted that Monica was not yet recovered from her divorce; that she'd been abused —battered?—by her husband.) His kisses were courtly, his caresses gentle. There was invariably an air of apology between him and Monica—a half-embarrassed sense that they were too old for such things yet too young to give them up.

One evening when they were having coffee at Monica's she brought up the subject, rather impulsively, of suicide. "Have you ever had any suicidal friends?" she asked Keith. Her voice was neutral enough so that he need not become alarmed, or take offense; he might answer casually if he wished.

He took his time replying. "Yes," he said finally, stroking his jaw, "—a close friend. My roommate at college. But I haven't thought of him in years."

"Why not?" Monica asked. She'd had several glasses of white wine at dinner and felt uncharacteristically bold. *Why not,* indeed.

"Steven and I were extremely close for years," Keith said. "We were at Choate together; then we roomed together at Virginia, as undergraduates, our junior and senior years. After graduation something happened to Steven and he eventually killed himself. A hunting 'accident' in the mountains. . . ." Keith was speaking in a slow flat voice, as if the words in his mouth had density, weight. He said: "Of course everyone knew Steven had been unhappy for years but it was hard to take it seriously because . . . because it had gone on for years, it had become a sort of psychic tic. He was morbid but he joked about it too. He was always joking, in fact. So if you took him at his word he was liable to turn mocking. And then it was all so frustrating and wearisome . . ."

Keith sounded faintly annoyed. Monica murmured, "How sad," and felt quite a fool, staring at the coffee mug in her hand. But she could not resist—why *should* she resist?—going on to ask why Keith's friend had committed suicide.

"Oh, as to 'why'—!" Keith said impatiently. "Do you think *they* know? It's all a sort of a harlequin routine—a sham—"

"A *sham?*"

"It's all so stupefyingly self-conscious. Any reason will do: a professional failure, a bad weekend, a love affair that hasn't worked out, childhood memories that aren't perfect. There isn't anything you can do if someone wants to kill himself. These people are incredibly stubborn and devious. They want to die and they're determined to die and it never has anything much to do with other people, or even with their own lives—their good or bad luck, whatever. There's something crippled and stunted about their souls." At this Keith paused; he had been speaking rather dramatically. He said, with an effort at a smile: "Basically they don't give a damn about other people. Which is why we resent them— *we* are the other people."

"I see," Monica said.

She was deeply moved by Keith's words; she felt tears gathering in her eyes. But for whom? For the lost Steven? For Keith himself, trembling with hurt and disappointment . . . ?

Then, in the next instant, he startled her with the perfunctory nature of his voice. As if giving counsel he said: "If you know anyone who's suicidal, Monica, I hope you will simply avoid him or her. Friendship with a person like that is a cul-de-sac—a kind of maze or labyrinth. Strength seems to flow from the healthy person to the unhealthy but it drains away, it doesn't do the slightest amount of good, it's a profitless situation all around." He paused; he took out a freshly laundered handkerchief and dabbed lightly at his mouth. "I hope you aren't thinking of someone in your family? I don't suppose it would be someone around here. . . ."

"I don't know," Monica said uneasily. Then she realized how ambiguous she sounded. "No, the person I'm thinking of is in North Africa as far as I know. Thousands of miles away. And we're out of contact."

Keith had been watching her closely. "Good," he said. "If you're wise you will steer clear of him—or her—whoever it is. And consider yourself fortunate."

"Oh yes," Monica said, "I do. I do consider myself fortunate."

And if the world's secret panels slid shut? and all became slick shadowless surface? and there remained no texture, no resistance? and she could not bring herself to mourn? and her life was a matter of going on—and on—and on?

6

THE HOUSE IN which Monica lived was not hers and never
would be but she spent a good deal of time working on it,
to give it the semblance of being hers. She felt greedy for
possession; for the corporeal fact of property; "real" estate.
She scoured—she sanded—she stripped wallpaper—she
painted floors and walls, even ceilings. (Why don't I help
you, Keith had suggested shyly, but Monica murmured excuses, Monica didn't want the man to lift a hand, she
feared that, if he imprinted himself upon the house even
minimally he would want to buy it, and move in with her.
He would want to marry her: wasn't that the natural next
step?)

Since she had to write letters home to prove to her parents that she *was* happy, she *was* busily absorbed in her
new life, Monica wrote at length about her teaching and
about her work—her physical labor—in her house. (That
it was not strictly speaking "her" house was an issue she
did not dwell upon.) She enclosed little sketches, floor
plans, cheery little progress reports that meant nothing
back in Wrightsville. Once on the telephone Monica's
mother had uttered the terrible words, "Well, Monica—it
is important to keep busy," and Monica had felt pierced to
the heart.

Still, her mother was right. She kept busy, busy.

Monica spent many hours cleaning the cellar. She wore a
filthy old jacket and gloves, and a scarf tied about her head
to protect her from cobwebs. As she raked up piles of foul-
smelling debris she thought, as if mesmerized, *How good,*

how healthy, this is real, this is absolute. Her breath steamed; the air was freezing but stagnant; below-ground, she kept imagining she heard the telephone ring . . . and ring and ring. She imagined she heard the back door (always kept locked) being forced open. She imagined she heard footsteps directly overhead. . . .

It's a man's world, one of the nurses had said, at the abortion clinic, years ago. It's a man's world: said sighingly, as one might make a reference to the weather, or the time of day. A man's world, *that* world, the fluorescent-lit disinfectant-smelling clinic, populated solely by women.

But why did Monica think of that remark now, so safely below-ground?

And why think of one of Sheila's pals breaking into her house, Eddy, or Buzz, or Grady, or Fitch, they'd forgotten Mary Beth long ago. They had never known Mary Beth at all. No, if someone broke into her house it would be a stranger, Monica supposed: a man she had never seen before, never even guessed at.

It was in the cellar, however, that Monica discovered a sheet of stained glass, amid a pile of debris stacked in a corner. The glass, lightly cracked in several places, measured about three feet by two and was a self-contained work of art: crimson, green, and turquoise panels framing a languorous, stylized *fin de siècle* lily, of the kind Klimt or Beardsley might have created. When it was scrubbed clean Monica was struck by its beauty and by her rare good luck in finding it. *This* too is an absolute, she thought in triumph, not knowing quite what she meant.

She placed the glass carefully in her kitchen window, facing south, so that it would catch the morning light. Her first instinct was to telephone Sheila, to call her over to examine it.

7

THEY WERE SO tirelessly good, so fatiguingly selfless, it was impossible not to admire them: James and Jill Starkie, the Glenkill chaplain and his devoted wife: James in a turtle-necked Highlander sweater of heather-gray and Jill in her orange embroidered hostess gown with a Mexican shawl draped dramatically about her shoulders. James exuded the rich scent of pipe tobacco, Jill a heady, perhaps too concentrated scent of Chanel No. 5. James was tall and thick-bodied and vibrant with good health and good Christian cheer, Jill was nervously exhilarated, visibly trembling with maternal solicitude, magnanimity, gaiety. Her greetings were all exclamations, breathy and urgent: How good to see you! How wonderful you look! How *kind* of you to come!

James Starkie's wide white-toothed smile was like a beacon of light, almost too dazzling. And his big hand, clasping Monica's, was capable of giving, for the briefest of instants, genuine pain. Jill's welcomes were gentler yet more alarmingly enveloping: she embraced, she nearly hugged, kissing Monica's cheek (and surely leaving a smear of crimson lipstick), she said with an air of subtle reproach, "It seems I *never* see you, Monica!"

Nearly every evening of the week the Starkies threw open their house on campus—"threw open" seemed the precise term—to a promiscuous gathering of students, faculty members, friends and acquaintances in Glenkill, visitors from out of town, professional colleagues. It was no ordeal for Jill Starkie to cook up a spaghetti supper for thirty or forty people—to spend an entire day preparing a buffet for sixty people—to send out invitations to one hundred people inviting them to sherry and cheese parties, open houses following football, soccer, basketball games in season. She loved an impromptu evening of supremely mismatched guests (a visiting theologian, the boys' swimming coach, a random assortment of students, the English Department secretary and her husband, a plumber) gathered about a roaring fire to drink hot chocolate and to eat, with some good-natured difficulty, roasted marshmallows. Somehow it had come about—*how* had it come about!— that Monica Jensen, being new to Glenkill, and unmarried, and therefore surely lonely, was often included in this ragtag assemblage of guests, telephoned at the last minute, alternately begged and bullied into accepting. Sometimes Jill behaved as if she were conferring a great honor on Monica by inviting her, sometimes she behaved as if Monica were conferring a great honor on *her*, by accepting. It was all dizzying—ecstatic—a whirlwind of names, embraces, handshakes, bungled introductions. (Jill frequently called Monica by the wrong name—Myra, Maura, Mona, and so forth—when introducing her to a large group of people. James invariably corrected her, with an edge to his voice, but raising a forefinger as if he had caught out one of his children in a naughty prank. And Jill then blushed, and begged Monica, squeezing her fingers, to forgive her: and it was all amusing, and rather appealing: "I just get so *rattled*, I muddle everybody's name, it isn't just *you*, Monica," Jill would say, "why, I know your name as well as I know my own!")

Everyone in Glenkill was fond of the Starkies. The boys, it was said, adored James: he really was a fantastic sort of chaplain for a preparatory school: so thoroughly and zestfully a *man*. And Jill too was prized for her unflagging warmth, her generosity, her air of slightly dizzy glamour. The ruder Glenkill boys sniggered behind her back, made the usual adolescent jokes, but most of them liked her very much, and basked in her indiscriminate maternal love. She was so unblinkingly and unapologetically a *Christian*—Monica had never met anyone quite like her. In a supremely casual tone Jill would introduce God or Jesus Christ into the conversation as if the presence of these deities in her home were altogether normal, nothing out of the ordinary. "Can't you just *feel* Jesus seated here with us tonight!—it's just the sort of group He would relate to!" Jill might suddenly exclaim; or, in a graver mood: "I can feel God's presence here, can't you?—as soon as James began grace—the 'spirit moving upon the waters'—" And it suddenly seemed to the Starkies' guests, glancing nervously at one another, that, perhaps, there *was* a supernatural being in their midst: the Starkies' most prized guest.

Jill had been tireless in her pursuit of Monica, since the start of the fall semester. She wanted, she said, to sit down and *talk* with Monica—Monica might come to lunch at her house—or tea—or they might drive to Philadelphia together, to spend an afternoon at the art museum "or the Rodin Museum—you must not miss *that*." But somehow this invitation never came about. And Monica did not encourage it—she was not *quite* so lonely, she thought, as to yearn for Jill Starkie's company.

Jill was in her late thirties but dressed and behaved like an older sister to her daughters. She had dyed her hair a flamboyant carrot color, and wore it fashionably curled; her eyebrows were penciled in dramatically; her lips shone with an opaque gloss; her clothes were unfailingly exotic—caftans, saris, sandals that laced to midcalf, long skirts in peasant hues and textures, hooded Icelandic wool coat-sweaters, Indian smocks of startlingly transparent muslin. Jill *was* glamorous without being at all attractive: the face beneath the theatrical makeup, inside the frizzed orange-red hair, was somewhat hard and plain. What fascinated

Monica about Jill was the woman's remarkable sense of herself—her idea of herself as privileged, bountiful, capable of lavishing blessings upon others—a kind of emissary for Christ, perhaps, or for the "Good News" of the Gospels. "To think that all these boys—these wonderful boys —these vulnerable yearning young souls!—are given over to our trust: to think that they look for guidance to *us!*" Jill once said, clasping her hands before her and staring at Monica. "Only think: only *think* of the situation—the opportunity—for saving souls, for changing lives, for doing *good*. James and I give thanks to God every day and every minute of our lives, that *we* are so blessed, in being at the Glenkill Academy!"

And though Monica recoiled from Jill's manner, and from the queer self-congratulatory nature of her words, she had to admit that there was truth to what Jill said. Teaching in this excellent school was a true privilege; being entrusted with such outstanding students—or, in fact, any students at all—was a remarkable opportunity.

"Isn't it a miracle, Monica?—our being here?—with *them?*" Jill said pleadingly; and Monica replied, embarrassed, "Yes, I suppose it is."

Sheila despised Jill Starkie, whom she called, simply, the chaplain's wife, and Monica had once amused Sheila by fantasizing a sordid private life for Jill: for wasn't she the stereotypical "happy" and "fulfilled" woman who, as you become acquainted with her, discloses, by degrees, appalling secrets . . . ? Miscarriages; bouts of mania and depression; a child or two hooked on drugs; a faithless husband, or, better yet, a husband who is secretly homosexual; an addiction to Librium or afternoon drinking. But, alas, nothing of the sort was disclosed: Jill proved supremely sunny, supremely *happy,* at all times, at any hour of the day, with never a lapse, never the slightest hint of weariness or self-doubt or cynicism. Here was a human being,

Monica thought critically, who truly *was* the person her appearance suggested.

"No doubt I could learn a good deal from her," Monica thought, "—but what would it be?"

One evening in late February, some time after Monica had learned that Sheila was away, she accepted a last-minute invitation to a potluck supper with the Starkies. She was somewhat distracted throughout the evening—but the evening went well—well enough—and then, after the meal, an astonishing event occurred, an incident *sui generis* which Monica was never to understand: Monica was helping to clear the table, found herself alone in the kitchen with James Starkie, they blundered into each other, laughing, slightly drunk, and with no warning James's enormous fingers closed about Monica's shoulders, and, in an outburst of sheerly animal ebullience, he loomed down to kiss her—pressing his wine-sweetened lips hard on hers, mashing them against hers, then withdrawing, turning quickly away, as if nothing had happened: just as Jill swept into the kitchen, splendid in her long orange gown, her hair slightly askew, her face flushed with joy. Of course Jill saw nothing, Jill guessed at nothing, and, afterward, Monica came to the conclusion that the kiss *was* nothing: James meant no more by it than he meant by one of his bone-aching handshakes, or his casual blessings.

And would he try to contact her, later?—Monica wondered uneasily.

And did she want him to do so, as a kind of diversion, at least?

No. Surely no. For the kiss had been a boy's kiss, and not a man's—sudden, rough, well-intentioned, forgettable.

8

Monica would not have cared to admit it but she had fallen into the habit of driving home by way of the Poor Farm Road. It meant an extra four miles but (as she told herself) the landscape was more interesting, more varied: hilly farmland interspersed with woods that ran out to the road, so that entering them, speeding into them, was vaguely disorienting, vaguely pleasurable, like rushing into a tunnel. Many of the tallest trees were pines, so that the forest, in midwinter, was as dark as it would be in summer. Often, after a heavy snowfall, it was even darker.

An eerie sensation, plunging into one of these stretches. Feeling her eyes begin to dilate at once, to adjust to the sudden change of light. Feeling as if . . . as if she might emerge in another part of the country . . . not in Bucks County, not on the Poor Farm Road that led past Sheila Trask's house, but in, perhaps, one of the isolated suvivalist areas . . . North Carolina, Montana, New Mexico . . . the "sand counties" of Wisconsin. Wild vistas, distant snowy mountain peaks, a lunar landscape pitiless in its frigid beauty; perhaps a choppy river running close beside the road. "And if I were to disappear no one would know where I had gone," Monica thought, a wave of chill pleasure breaking over her. "*She* would never know."

But she simply continued along her route, emerging from the woods and into the open, returned to much that was familiar and should have been comforting. Of course there was no reason for Monica to be driving along the Poor Farm Road, wasn't she trespassing?—taking a chance? This was not her road but Sheila's. She felt a sub-

159

tle dread, a fascinated dread, as, driving fairly fast, she approached one of the road's snaky turns; its awkward dips and ruts; its narrow crumbling concrete bridges. After a snowstorm the road was hardly more than a single lane, unplowed for days. . . .

Sheila Trask was widely known to be a restless driver. Especially on the Poor Farm Road, "her" road. She took the curves at high speeds, she absentmindedly swung out into the left lane, she did an alarming amount of juggling behind the wheel as she tried to fish a pack of cigarettes out of her pocket, find a matchbook, light a match. . . . Sometimes too she drove when her mind wasn't clear. . . .

Monica resisted the impulse to speed up. To match Sheila. She passed familiar fields, woods, a few scattered farmhouses, the remains of the old poorhouse, and then, suddenly, Edgemont itself—looking, in the late afternoon light, rather grim and weathered at the end of its long snowy drive. It was absurd and pretentious, Monica thought, for a house to have a name; as if Sheila Trask, or Morton Flaxman, were of noble birth. The house too was pretentious, a country squire's mansion, fieldstone, stucco, brick, slate roofs and enormous chimneys, an inappropriate stately air—inappropriate for the rural setting. Sheila should sell the property and move away, Monica thought. It was wasteful and extravagant and pointless for a single woman, and a woman of such a temperament, to own a place like Edgemont; to live alone in the country; with her neighbors covertly watching her, and passing judgment.

Little changed about Edgemont, day following day. Someone picked up the mail; someone was using the driveway; but very few persons seemed to be around. Monica, driving by, could not prevent herself from slowing her car . . . to look hard, hungrily, bitterly up the long driveway. She could not see, of course, the carriage house and the parking area but she supposed that Sheila's old station wagon was there, in its usual position. The carriage house would be locked up tight, most likely; the snow about its doorstep would be undisturbed.

9

BUT THEN, ONE day in late March, there was the station wagon—Sheila's car, and no other—parked in Monica's driveway.

And there was Sheila herself, strolling in the pasture close by, hands stuck in her pockets, a cigarette in her mouth.

Monica drove into her driveway; braked her car to a jolting stop; sat trembling; staring. Sheila raised her hand in a formal gesture of greeting and came slowly forward . . . slowly, as if she too were frightened.

The women greeted each other, they shook hands, they smiled awkwardly, spoke a few words, fell silent. Monica's head was pounding and Sheila herself was visibly agitated.

Finally Sheila said in a low, rapid voice, "You aren't exactly overjoyed to see me, are you."

Monica laughed nervously. *"Aren't* I—?"

Sheila was regarding her with a sly shy half-smile, her head turned to one side as if she couldn't quite bring herself to look directly at Monica. Her voice was elated, accusing, "And I've been gone for so long: and you *haven't* missed me."

Monica denied it, laughing again. Her face had gone strangely hot; her eyes were burning; she was nearly overcome by an impulse to strike Sheila with her fist—a child's greeting, playful, yet hard enough to hurt. Yes, in play: but hard enough to hurt.

"I don't blame you," Sheila said, expelling a cloud of

smoke in a sudden heavy sigh. "I would have come back earlier, you know—except—I was afraid of your anger—your judgment. Yet I *don't* blame you," she said in a musing voice.

Monica was no longer certain what they were talking about. She said, rather too briskly, "Well—it's good to see you back. To have you back. How was your stay in Morocco? Did you—"

But Monica's words trailed off into silence, as if she had lost the thread of her own remark; and Sheila did not seem to hear. She was picking a bit of tobacco off her tongue, flicking it away. Sheila said vaguely, "And how have you been, here? I suppose you've been—working—teaching— And seeing people—"

"Yes," said Monica. "A good many people."

Sheila was dressed extravagantly in jodhpurs, riding boots, a burgundy wool cape that fell rakishly to her ankles. Her thick hair was gathered into a casual twist at the back of her head; stray wisps blew across her forehead and into her eyes. She was a striking woman even in this stark wintry glare, which threw its bluish light upward, shadowing the eyes, emphasizing tucks and creases about the mouth, draining the skin of its color. Lean and angular and impatient, with the air of being sharp as a knife blade; a curious blend of audacity and humility—even self-abasement; Sheila Trask with her black rapacious eyes, the too-heavy brows, the fleshy mouth with its uncertain smile. Monica remembered having thought, in Sheila's studio, beneath that pitiless skylight, that beauty is after all only a matter of light; of gradations of light; degrees of seeing. But now, staring at Sheila, lost in contemplation of Sheila, she realized that Sheila's beauty had nothing to do with accidents of light, or gradations of clarity, or Monica's own rapt vision. It was there, Sheila was there, supremely herself.

Yet she was ill at ease, visibly nervous. She said in a faltering voice, "I suppose you detest the very sight of me," and of course Monica replied at once, "Don't be ridiculous," then added, more sharply, *"Why* should I detest you?—you take yourself too seriously."

PART IV

The Labyrinth

1

SHEILA'S PRESENTS, FROM Morocco: a pair of silver earrings, finely wrought, that fell in exquisite loops and spirals halfway to Monica's shoulder; a pale green scarf stitched with gold thread in arabesque designs; a necklace of chunky amethysts, topaz stones, and ornamental shells of various sizes. While Sheila watched closely Monica slipped the heavy necklace over her head, fingering the stones and shells, frowning in admiration. The necklace *was* exotic, she felt transformed simply by wearing it. . . . The shells resembled snail shells but they were delicately striated, and gave off a pungent odor, not at all unpleasant, that reminded Monica of brackish water. It crossed her mind too—hazily—the hour was late, she had had several glasses of red wine—that the shells might not have been thoroughly cleaned, that particles of decayed flesh remained inside, bits of nameless sea creatures, perhaps poisonous, unwise to wear so close to her face.

"Beautiful," Sheila said, staring.

Nothing has changed, Monica told herself.

Then, in triumph: *everything* has changed.

Now she would be cautious—*she* would be in control.

Monica listened closely to Sheila's talk of Morocco, Monica listened to discover what, precisely, had happened there; what secret adventures Sheila had had, if any. (But surely that was the purpose of running away?—to have adventures, secret or otherwise? And to speak of them, to hint of them, upon returning home?)

North Africa was a place of elemental facts, Sheila said.

Americans thought it primitive, unnerving. No doubt it was: whatever "primitive" meant. The air so remarkably dry, the sun so direct and forceful, so whitely hot, powerful . . . you spent a good deal of time watching the sky, with a sensation that something would happen there at any minute; that whatever happened on earth, even to you, must be inconsequential. A sort of communal dream.

Of course, Sheila said briskly, the North Africans, for all their religious devotion, are hardly mystics. Allah may be a mysterious deity inhabiting the sky but they themselves are nothing if not immediate, canny, physical . . . supremely physical.

The men, at least.

As for the women: Sheila hadn't in fact become acquainted with any women Moslems. (There was a saying, which Sheila repeated with a bitter sort of zest: A woman goes out only three times during her life—once when she is born and leaves her mother's womb, once when she marries and leaves her father's house, and once when she dies and leaves this world.)

What about the men, Monica asked.

Sheila ignored her question, which was in fact uttered in so low a voice it might reasonably not have been heard. She went on to speak of the architecture in Tangier—the painting done by Moslems ("a sort of Abstract Expressionism, quite haunting")—the beauty of the Mediterranean—the cypresses—Spain across the strait—the Sahara ("Do you know Hassan is fighting a Sahara war?—to put down a rebellion of some sort, he says, but it's really for reasons of greed")—the Moslem religion in which men and women live their lives with a continuous reference to Allah, to Allah as the arbiter and measure of all things ("a crime against another person is only a crime if it offends Allah as well—and nothing greatly matters that does not matter to *him"*)—the sense of isolation, heartrending solitude, which Sheila found virtually everywhere, even in the most crowded streets and bazaars.

"Still, I grew to like it. I saw that that was why I'd come—not to be alone with myself but to be alone," Sheila said.

Monica, eyeing her closely, felt a prick of annoyance; perhaps of jealousy.

And was Sheila telling the truth?—did the woman ever speak truthfully, or only improvisationally? She had mentioned earlier, with a childlike sort of boastfulness, that, in Morocco, she'd gained back the eight or ten pounds she had lost before Christmas; she had gained back some of her "muscle tone"—this said while playfully gripping her upper arm, and then her thigh. But Monica did not see any significant change in Sheila other than the faintly golden tan, the olive-golden tan, which was already beginning to fade.

"But weren't you in a circle of some sort," Monica asked skeptically, "—expatriated Americans, Parisians?— artists? Weren't you staying in a friend's villa on the Mediterranean?"

Sheila made an impatient dismissive gesture as if such factors, mere people, counted not at all. "Some of the time, yes," she said. "And I quite liked them—most of them. I *like* people, you know. But I went away by myself too, after the second week. They warned me it was dangerous—a woman, alone, there—a 'Christian' woman—a heretic—but it wasn't precisely as a *woman* I traveled; and nothing serious ever happened."

Monica stared at her. "Nothing serious—? But what *did* happen?"

"I'll tell you another time," Sheila said. "In any case it isn't important. What mattered to me was being alone; being there; seeing something in the landscape, in the light,

I'd never seen before." She spoke slowly, meditatively. "Yes, it was new. I don't think I'm deceiving myself. A way of seeing, an angle of . . . vision, you could say; a certain rhythm to seeing, as you acquire, in a foreign country, a rhythm of hearing. And now that I'm back home I don't intend to lose it."

2

SHEILA WAS BACK at work; hard at work; and meant to be a recluse, until the paintings were finished.

But she telephoned Monica at least once a day, usually in the early evening, to inquire how things were going for Monica. *(She* had no news at all—nothing to report.)

So Monica was obliged to speak of committee meetings, lunches with colleagues, classes that went unusually well, or disappointed ("Now they've got it into their heads that Mark Twain was a racist"); an awkward hour-long conference with the parents of one of her poorer students. Matters that could not possibly be of interest to another person became, at such times, highly significant; even emblematic; for all that Monica did and said and thought seemed to represent, in Sheila's imagination, the actions of a person of supreme though mysterious importance.

"Why are you asking me this—?" Monica broke off one evening, in embarrassment, and Sheila must have been so startled she couldn't reply at first; then she said, "I suppose—because—if I don't ask—*you* won't tell."

Nothing has changed, Monica thought,—except my control.

For she meant, this time, to be in control.

She was already, was she not?—in control.

Yes: in control.

Control.

She quite liked the word, its classy air.

Control. *Control.*

"This time," she said, "—mine."

171

3

THEN IT WAS mentioned, as if casually, incidentally, that Sheila might postpone her show another time.

She couldn't bear the pressure, she said.

She hated all she'd done. And there was no time to remedy it.

"I'm at an impasse," she said, lightly mocking. (Monica having told her of Keith Renwick's use of the word.) "I'm about to have a 'crisis.'"

"Go back to work," Monica might say, breezily, to disguise the concern she felt; or, variously, "Take off a few hours, for God's sake—go for a ride on Parsifal—come over here for a drink."

Sheila resumed the subject, not altogether enthusiastically, of Sherrill Ann and Mary Beth: their pals out at the Swedesboro Inn and Walt's must be wondering where they are, right? and where *are* they?

Monica thought of herself in that filthy restroom, squatting over a stained toilet seat, urinating in hot shamed splashes while the bartender and "Sherrill Ann" stood guard a few feet away, on the other side of a door that wouldn't lock. The tastes of draft beer, stale potato chips, pizza . . . the sound of country-and-western music blaring from the jukebox . . . the smell of cigarette smoke, hair oil. And there was Fitch's face raw with hatred: an emotion Monica had well understood at the time.

"Was the name 'Mary Beth'?" Monica asked suddenly. "Wasn't it—'Marie Beth'?—'Merrill Beth'? I can't remember."

"God," Sheila said, puzzled, "I don't know. I thought it was 'Mary Beth'—wasn't it?"

"I remember your name, 'Sherrill Ann,' but I don't remember my own," Monica said.

"'Mary Beth,' I think."

"'Mary Beth'?—if you say so."

She would not consent to go drinking with Sheila, even to the most innocuous of the taverns; she was finished, she said, with that sort of thing forever. "Then I'll be obliged to go alone," Sheila said.

Monica said, *"No."*

But Sheila evidently did go out drinking, alone, once or twice, perhaps more, hinting the day after that she'd had quite an adventure, quite . . . an interesting adventure; complaining half-humorously of being hung over. One night, she woke Monica from a sound sleep by telephoning at two in the morning from Hedy's Café, where, she said, she'd met an extremely interesting man who had an extremely interesting buddy, both of them state troopers (off-duty), both good-looking in their own way. Wouldn't Mary Beth like to come join them? "You're drunk," Monica said angrily, banging down the receiver.

Next day when Monica returned from Glenkill she found in her mailbox a skillful little crayon and charcoal drawing, an act of contrition on Sheila's part, evidently. It was a highly stylized likeness of Monica herself, all suggestive smudges and blurs and cryptic shadows; an unsmiling likeness, indeed. *La Belle Dame Sans . . .* was the inscription.

4

As IF NOTHING had changed, Sheila began to drop by Monica's house, always with the happy excuse of being in the neighborhood; driving to Glenkill on an errand, perhaps. She even appeared once or twice at school, to see if Monica might happen to be free for lunch: no? yes? At a reception at the Greenes' in early April—held to honor a visiting alumnus, a wealthy Boston manufacturer—Sheila showed up late, but made a strong impression, giving no quarter to the guest of honor in his good-natured denunciation of modern art. (For naturally it turned out that the gentleman knew nothing apart from a few names—Pollock, Rothko, Warhol?—Mondrian?) Another evening, in a small group gathered for dinner at the Chinese restaurant, Sheila dominated the conversation, speaking of ways of seeing that were conditioned by ways of political thinking. "If you don't think well you can't see well—it's as simple as that," Sheila said. The men in the party, Monica's colleagues, were quite clearly attracted by Sheila without knowing how to talk to her. Did one challenge her, head-on?—or listen closely, and agree? How was it possible to get her unqualified attention?—her respect?

One of the young men asked Monica the next day if Sheila Trask was always like that.

"Always like what?" Monica said coldly.

To Sheila she said she thought it unwise, imprudent, for her to say such things—such wild vehement visionary things—in front of people who weren't artists and who weren't even intellectuals, but who would repeat her re-

174

marks, muddle them, even make fun of them. "Christ," said Sheila, blinking as if dazed, "—what did I *say*? I don't remember." She ran her hands through her hair, squinting at Monica. "Morton used to be like that—he talked too much when he was talking at all—the rest of the time, he couldn't be bothered, he'd just *sit*. I know I say the most contemptible sort of bullshit if I'm a little high— why don't you kick me under the table, shut me up—I'm fucking *sorry* if I embarrassed you."

Monica was touched, moved. She said, relenting: "You don't embarrass me at all, Sheila. You know that. It's just that these other people don't understand you and they're alerted to listening for things they can repeat, to add a cubit or two to their height, bragging that they know you."

"Yes. Right. Just kick me under the table," Sheila said, "if it happens again."

Again, suddenly, Sheila was drinking; again, smoking too heavily.

And taking amphetamines—or so Monica gathered.

(In Tangier, Sheila said, she'd had some marvelous hashish—it had done her head good. But she'd been too cowardly to smuggle any back with her and unless she wanted to make a trip to New York City she couldn't get anything of that quality again.)

Drunk, or high, loquacious, bright and brittle and un-nervingly cheerful, Sheila sometimes said that she knew she was an artist—a genuine artist; and sometimes said that she was "probably finished." At such times she spoke in a flat elegiac voice. She was through with her career; finished, burnt out, dead. Monica challenged her at once, Monica tried to laugh her out of her moods, but Sheila was adamant. "Careers die just like people," she said. "Yet the wheels keep spinning. The cogs keep moving, locking and grinding in place. The old wheezing heart."

And Monica would protest; and Sheila would fall stubbornly silent.

They were shy of touching each other, even of drawing close by accident. Monica recalled that hissed admonition of Sheila's—*I don't care to be touched*—and stiffened, herself, if, in one of her more effusive states, Sheila drew too close. She was conscious of Sheila's warm breath, Sheila's scent. The fact that Sheila took up so much more space than her fairly thin frame required.

Weeks passed before Sheila made any reference to Christmas; to Monica's visit home. "How was your family?" she asked guardedly.

"Very well," Monica said. "Very well indeed."

"I thought that was where you'd gone—to Indiana."

"Yes," said Monica.

She was waiting for Sheila to apologize; but even as she waited (thinking with an angry beating heart of her pleas to Sheila through that door—her pathetic attempts at humor, coercion) she knew that Sheila would never say a word. Sheila, hiding on the other side of a locked door, slightly crouched, head bowed, breathing hoarsely through her mouth. Sheila listening to *her* and saying not a word.

"Yes," said Monica, "the visit went very well indeed. Except they put pressure on me to come back to Indiana, to teach there."

"I don't blame them," Sheila said neutrally. "If they love you they must want you closer. It's a long distance away, after all."

Monica said nothing, nor did she look directly at Sheila.

"Suppose you'd died. . . ." she said suddenly, in a whisper. "Suppose I'd come too late and you had. . . ."

Sheila turned away; Sheila said in a vague drifting

voice, "Yes I *thought* that was where you'd gone, home to visit your family. It was Christmas after all. . . ."

"Yes," Monica said angrily. "Christmas."

And the subject was never mentioned again.

5

MONICA'S TEACHING WAS going well, Monica's first year was quite a success, or would surely be, at the end of the term; yet she worried; wondered; calculated. What sort of future did she have at Glenkill? why hadn't she been offered a three-year contract instead of a one-year renewal (as it was called)?—the rumor being that one of her young male colleagues *had* been offered a contract of this sort, and had signed up gratefully.

Was her status as a divorced woman a mark against her, she wondered.

Was there something perhaps unwise—imprudent—naive—about her very enthusiasm for teaching? She recalled an admonition of Harold's that one's colleagues invariably objected to too much enthusiasm: it put them in a bad light.

Sheila suggested that Monica was being exploited at the Glenkill Academy, by Greene and his "gang." He was notorious, Sheila said. Pushing his junior faculty to the limit, expecting them to work for virtually nothing, paying them in school camaraderie, dinner parties, free tickets to basketball games. One big happy family, the Glenkill staff. One big happy family with Daddy at the head.

"You could almost do as well, penny by penny and hour by hour, working as a barmaid," Sheila said, not very tactfully.

"But where else could I go," Monica said lightly, "—where else could I be exploited in such congenial surroundings? By such attractive well-bred people?"

* * *

Another time, Sheila told Monica that she owed it to herself to take sick days off, now and then. As everyone else did. She was foolish to teach week after week without a break, as if it were to her credit, a measure of her stoicism. Also, Sheila had to drive to New York City on business and couldn't bear the thought of driving alone and wouldn't Monica like to join her. . . .

"No thank you," Monica said.

Then, reconsidering: "Why don't you wait until Saturday? I could leave by nine-thirty. I could never forgive myself if you had an accident, driving all that distance alone."

"I don't intend to have an accident of any kind," Sheila said stiffly. "But I'd certainly appreciate your company."

"It's a long drive," Monica said.

"A long dull drive," Sheila said, "—alone."

In the car Sheila spoke of her Tangier adventures, her "two or three" Arab lovers, her meeting with her old friend Henri.

"Ah—'Henri'!" Monica said in a neutral voice.

"Henri's secret—which isn't of course a secret to *me*—is that he's gay, masquerading as straight, and women exist solely to prove to him that he *is* straight when in fact—as Henri well knows—he *isn't*." Sheila glanced at Monica, as if Monica might be drawn into sympathetic laughter; but Monica stared ahead at the turnpike traffic. "Still, he always wants to try; and he always fools me; he's so *sincere*. And so attractive. The son of a bitch *is* attractive, don't you think?—you saw his picture. But it was all very disappointing—very frustrating—and afterward he showed me a snapshot of a baby—his baby!—olivish skin but very fair hair and eyes. *Henri's baby!* But the joke, Monica, is," Sheila said, speaking now rapidly, excitedly, and paying very little attention to her driving, "—you won't believe it but the joke is, Henri wasn't involved at all, not involved with any woman, I mean not as such, the mother is a French lesbian, a poet, she's well-known evidently but *I* had never heard of her, she'd been impregnated by a lesbian 'midwife,' as they call them, using Henri's sperm—semen—isn't it wild?—freaky-wild?—he told me proudly he masturbated into a bottle and gave the bottle to the midwife and *she* prepared a spray solution or a syringe solution, or whatever—I was laughing so hard by then I couldn't hear—isn't it funny!—Henri, a father!—and anyway, Monica, they squirt it up into themselves and if it connects, it connects, and they have their babies *sans* men, and they're 'married' most of the time—the women, the lesbians—and they're said to be devoted mothers. Can you believe it! Isn't it wild! *Can* you believe it!"

Monica was watching the turnpike; Monica's teeth were on edge.

"Jesus, *can* you believe it!" Sheila said, thumping the steering wheel. She was laughing in short soundless spasms. "And poor Henri was so proud, he kept boasting, 'My son, look,' and I thought of him masturbating into a bottle, and I *couldn't* stop laughing. . . ."

"Watch where you're going," Monica said sharply.

Sheila jerked the wheel and eased her car back into her own lane; it had been drifting to the left. "I *am* watching," she said. But it seemed that she really couldn't stop laughing—tears were streaming down her face, her expression was pained, contorted—and in the end Monica had to insist upon taking over. "I'm all right, I'm perfectly all right," Sheila said, choking, sobbing, wiping at her eyes, but she surrendered the car readily enough to Monica.

Afterward Monica said: "I don't know that it's all that funny. It seems rather touching. As long as the child never knows. . . ."

But this set Sheila off into peals of laughter again. She pounded at her knees, yelped and choked with hilarity. And after a while Monica joined in, Monica couldn't help herself. It *was* funny, somehow.

6

Now I am in control, Monica thought cautiously.

Now I know precisely what I am doing; what the perimeters of friendship must be.

By degrees, however, Monica found herself spending more and more time at Edgemont. For a while Sheila wanted her to visit her studio every afternoon; not to praise, or to make suggestions, but simply to look, in silence. ("It makes a tremendous difference to me," Sheila admitted, "—to think that you'll be dropping by. Just, you know, to look. To register that I exist and the paintings exist.") Often Monica drove there directly from school, to have supper with Sheila, then to return home to her own work. Saturdays, she spent most of the afternoon at Sheila's. And Sundays were unofficially set aside as one of their days together: she had to explain to Keith that she was never free, Sundays.

She never stayed the night at Edgemont, however. No matter how late she was in getting home, she never gave in to Sheila's repeated invitation to spend the night. ("I have a place of my own, Sheila," she said; and Sheila said, making a joke of it, "Why not have two places of your own . . . ?")

Monica was upset to discover how irresponsible Sheila Trask was in terms of practical life. There were desk drawers, cabinet drawers, even kitchen cupboards stuffed with bills (paid? unpaid? long forgotten); there were letters never opened (from Internal Revenue, Merrill Lynch, one or another of Sheila's banks, money men, attorneys); there

182

were requests of various kinds (would Sheila Trask be interested in a teaching position, or a position as artist-in-residence, would Sheila Trask be interested in being interviewed on television, on radio, in a national arts magazine) never answered. "How can you live like this!" Monica said, genuinely shocked. And Sheila, stricken, put her hands over her ears in a childish gesture. "Don't tell me. Don't frighten me," she begged.

Nothing to be done, then, but that Monica Jensen take over. To the degree to which she could spare the time.

And the problems, the vexations, were so close at hand: Sheila's cleaning woman was incompetent, or lazy, or deliberately dishonest; the boy who groomed Parsifal did a poor job of it, so that—as Monica learned to her amazement—Sheila herself had fallen into the habit of doing most of the work, without wishing, or daring, to say anything to the boy; the man who cleaned her septic tank (Roman Valentino was his unlikely name) had charged her $450, approximately three times too much. (Monica learned this by simply making a few telephone calls.) The Edgarsville roofing company had quoted so absurdly high an estimate, for repairs on the roof of the house, Sheila hadn't wanted to have the work done; nor had she gotten around to calling in other companies, for other estimates. It maddened her, she said, to be cheated; yet she felt resigned, listless. Morton was always being cheated and so it was quite natural that she was being cheated but what could she do about it. . . .

Sheila's fatalism in these matters angered Monica; the women fell to quarreling. "It's all so petty, so soul-numbing *petty*," Sheila said, "—let the sons of bitches cheat me if they want to," and Monica said, exasperated, "Don't be ridiculous, that's just what they are counting on, don't be *stupid*." So Monica examined the bills, the receipts, the letters, Monica examined Sheila's checking account (she seemed to have three), Monica made telephone calls, spoke briskly and assertively as she would never have spoken merely on her own behalf. (For who was Monica Jensen set beside "Sheila Trask"?) She derived a genuine pleasure from redressing outrageous wrongs, informing local tradesmen that their bills were exorbitant and would they please submit legitimate bills; otherwise, they may as well strike the account from their books.

There was the matter, more crucially, of Sheila's impending show. (Postponed now until May 17, the last possible date for the season.) Calls came daily from Sheila's gallery, from both the owner and the manager, was Sheila going to be ready on time? was Sheila all right? why wouldn't Sheila come to the phone? Numberless arrangements had to be made: invitations mailed, the brochure's galleys proofread by the artist, prices for the paintings settled, last-minute contacts made with the media. A champagne opening, of course, but Sheila *must* be there. ("I promise that she'll be there," Monica said with more certainty than she felt.)

With Monica so often at Edgemont Sheila was spared the necessity of talking on the telephone, an ordeal she dreaded. More and more, lately, since returning from North Africa, she was developing an aversion to the telephone; an almost pathological hatred of it. "I'm so grateful to you, Monica," she said; and Monica said impatiently, "I'm not doing these things for you, actually, I'm doing them for the sake of your paintings, and because I can't bear the thought of so many people taking advantage of you. I want them to know," she said, "there's someone here who is in charge."

7

SHEILA HAD GOOD days in her studio but they were balanced—in her private cosmology they were *necessarily* balanced—by bad days. Heights were followed by depths; exhilaration by depression. Yet she wasn't, she insisted, clinically ill: "I've been through all that before," she said mysteriously.

It was Monica's task, Monica's privilege, to help Sheila maintain an emotional equilibrium: an activity that took a great deal of her time but was in itself exhilarating. Walking a tightrope, high above the ground. Eyes fixed resolutely ahead, arms outspread for balance. The trick being not to look down; not ever to look down.

Monica had dropped her study-discussion group, that met on Thursday evenings; she made her excuses—vague, sincerely apologetic, guilty—to Keith; of course she had no time for swimming in Olcottsville; she had systematically pared back her life to teaching, and those academic meetings from which she could not reasonably absent herself, and her involvement with Sheila Trask. It was of paramount importance that the paintings be finished, the show properly hung. And the arrangements, the numerous arrangements, yet to be made . . . !

Because Sheila would far rather paint than eat, on her good days, Monica had to keep a close watch on her. She kept herself going for hours—eight, ten, twelve—on black coffee and amphetamines; she explained impatiently that she hadn't time for sitting down to eat and she hadn't any appetite in any case unless—unless Monica kept her company, Monica prepared the food, there *was* something special about the food Monica prepared. (And it was true, Monica had a flair for preparing unusual concoctions with the blender, experimenting, as she said, improvising, with exotic soups that never failed to intrigue Sheila: yogurt with shrimp and dill, puréed apple with curry, mulligatawny, cauliflower with onion and carrot, thyme, fresh-ground black pepper, in a strong chicken broth. She had to eat anyway, Monica told herself, she would have to prepare dinner at home, so why not in Sheila's handsome kitchen at Edgemont?—amidst the copper utensils, the blue and white ceramic tile, the broad windows overlooking a splendid sweep of land.)

Even when Monica worked hard to entice her, however, Sheila sometimes couldn't eat: she sat at the table, trying, her forehead damp with perspiration, trying *trying* to lift a fork or a spoon, her shoulders hunched inward, the cloth of her shirt pressed slightly against her breasts, showing only faintly the outline of the small breasts, the tiny hard nipples. Please eat, Monica begged, you must eat, Monica said severely, soup, omelettes, cheese and French bread, a lavish green salad filled with things Sheila loved, or had once loved, and eaten greedily. You must eat, Monica said, sitting across the table from her friend, watching,—you'll break my heart if you don't eat! she said, making a joke of it. But Sheila simply couldn't. Her stomach had closed, she said, her throat had closed, she felt no more attraction for food than she'd feel for chunks of paper or cardboard, nothing had any taste, she was frightened of becoming nauseated if she swallowed a few mouthfuls, please wouldn't Monica understand?

"Yes," Monica said, slowly, staring at Sheila, "—I understand. But my heart is broken just the same!"

* * *

So she joked about the situation, she teased and cajoled and went away hurt, furious, baffled, worried. (Should she call Sheila's doctor in Philadelphia? *Should* she insist that Sheila make an appointment to see him?—as if Sheila could be talked into anything of the kind.)

One day Monica happened to find, amidst a pile of bills and receipts in one of Sheila's drawers, an astounding document: a bill from Argus Investigative Services of Greater Manhattan, for $1,200, dated December of the previous year, and stamped PAID.

For some minutes Monica simply sat there, staring.

Argus Investigative Services. . . .

December of the previous year. . . .

Then she snatched up the receipt and ran over to the carriage house, ran up the stairs to Sheila's studio, half-sobbing in her fury, muttering under her breath, How dare you, how *dare* you, bitch, liar, she slammed into the room where Sheila was squatting before one of her canvases, brush in hand, she thrust the slip of paper at Sheila, into Sheila's dazed face, she began to scream, suddenly she was screaming, she was sobbing, "How dare you, how could you be so contemptible, so *vulgar*—this is so *vulgar*—" It was a measure of Sheila's odd blank resigned state that she made no attempt to defend herself against Monica's sudden frenzy: Monica slapped her, Monica even punched her on the shoulder, knocking her off balance: "Sheila, for Christ's sake, how *could* you!—how *could* you!"

Though Sheila could not have known what was wrong, she crouched guiltily, protecting her face with her arms, hunched like a small frightened child.

"How *could* you—" Monica cried a final time.

The frenzy had burnt itself out as suddenly as it had flared up. She was standing over Sheila, panting, sobbing; she felt as if she were on the very brink of madness . . . that she might do, and be allowed to do, something irreparable.

But the attack was over. The studio was quiet except for the women's harsh frightened breathing.

(And this incident was never again mentioned by either of the women. In her fury Monica crumpled the yellow receipt and threw it down, and, afterward, when she was alone, Sheila must have picked it up to examine it; but she never mentioned the "Argus Investigative Services" to Monica, and she certainly never apologized.

Very likely Sheila simply forgot, as the wisest and most practical of all procedures.)

8

MONICA, DISGUSTED, SMARTING with hurt and anger, stayed away from Edgemont for a day or two, Monica had after all (she told herself) her own life; and when she saw Sheila again she was alarmed at the change in her... wondering perhaps if it was her fault.

Sheila did look sick; vague and dazed and exhausted.

Her skin was a dull dead white, yet mottled, as if with teenage acne; the soft flesh about her eyes had grown puffy. In her speedy state (*speedy* being Sheila's own term) she gave off an unnerving radiant heat, sheer energy; in her other state (for which there was no appropriate term) her voice was slurred and her bodily movements uncoordinated.

"She's killing herself," Monica thought, staring.

And then: "She will *not* kill herself."

Sheila quite saw the humor of the situation, Sheila wanted no particular pity, out of self-respect, she said, and to do her small bit toward purifying the world, she really *ought* to slash her wrists: but she couldn't spare the time.

"Do you think that's amusing!" Monica said, "—I don't think that's amusing."

Sheila said defensively, avoiding Monica's gaze, "Look: in my family suicide isn't that significant. My mother allowed herself to die in a way that wasn't altogether 'natural' yet wasn't a melodramatic gesture of any kind, it was in fact ruled an accidental death, sparing us a good deal of nuisance; and no suicide note. One of my uncles died by simply blowing most of his brains out at the age of forty-nine, and two of my cousins killed themselves, no, please,

189

don't look so distressed, as you can see it *isn't* that significant, it's simply a way of asserting control at the proper time. When you've lived through all there is for you to live through, when you're burnt out, thoroughly, and the mere notion of returning to life, and doing it all again, the seasons, the years, the decades, O dear Christ. . . . When you're balked, nullified, stalled, it isn't a significant gesture, it isn't at all emotional, it's just something, you know, you *do*. And then it's over."

"Except of course it isn't," Monica said in a low trembling voice.

Sheila made an irritated dismissive gesture.

Sheila slouched out of the room, and refused to discuss the matter further.

Sheila did not trouble to reply when Monica called after her: "Except of course it *isn't*—you know very well that it *isn't*."

"If you cut down on your smoking," Monica said severely. "And your drinking. Those God-damned pills of yours."

"Yes," said Sheila.

"Are you listening?—are you going to try?"

"Oh yes," said Sheila, hiding her face in her hands.

Then there was the day, a Friday, at the end of a spectacularly busy week for Monica, when Sheila became possessed by the idea of joining a contingent of women—artists, writers, educators—who were going to China for six weeks, leaving the first of May. Anything, she said, to get out of Edgemont—out of her studio—out of her *head*.

The invitation from China had come to Sheila Trask by way of the State Department, many months before; she had of course turned it down without a second thought. (To be precise, she tossed the letter into a drawer without troubling to reply. "We can get perfectly good Chinese food right here in Glenkill," she told Monica, "—why the hell travel so *far*.") Now, however, she telephoned Washington a half-dozen times, she telephoned a liaison person in New York City, to see if arrangements could be made for her after all. It was an emergency! She wanted, she said, to immerse herself in Chinese culture. That inhospitable Peking climate of which she'd read—prolonged cold well into the spring, dust storms, aridity, life lived close to the bone—a region where individuality did not exist (except perhaps as pathology) and where the State swallowed everyone up and where there was not (for how could there be?) any margin for personal anguish and personal desire.

Anguish and desire, Sheila argued—aren't they identical?

And perhaps there would be a Chinese analogue, a sister of the soul, a "Sheila Trask" in that world: Sheila herself but totally transformed, purged of her failings, her sins.

"She could teach me a good deal," Sheila said wildly. "If it isn't too late. A sister—there—*there*—on the other side of the world—if it isn't too late—"

Fortunately, nothing came of Sheila's sudden flurry of interest.

By the time one of her calls to the cultural exchange office in Washington was returned, she had changed her mind—it *was* an absurd desperate ploy. And she was in the midst of rethinking the last of her paintings, she was greatly excited, she couldn't be disturbed: would Monica handle the call, would Monica explain?

Monica would, Monica did.

9

SUDDENLY, IN EARLY May, Sheila decided to give a dinner party.

She was tired, she said, teasingly, of hillbilly truckers with no last names; she ached for some social life, a little adventure of the kind she and Morton had frequently had amongst the local gentry.

"You're being preposterous," Monica said.

"You can't mean it," Monica said.

Sheila laughed, Sheila ran her hands through her hair zestfully.

"But you're first on my guest list," she said, reaching out as if to poke Monica, or to pinch—though she did neither, "—unless of course you decline. Yes? No?"

. More soberly she told Monica that she hadn't given a party of this kind—a genuine party—a *dinner* party—in years. When Morton was in the right phase he quite enjoyed these parties, he thought them the reverse of real life, like photograph negatives. The local gentry, not an artist among them; that is, not a serious artist; just as the farmers were all gentlemen farmers and country squires, playing at a rural life, keeping herds of useless Brahman cattle simply for the look of them, transforming meadows into putting greens, that sort of thing. She wanted to cook for an entire day, seriously. She wanted, she said, to wear a long dress and to be a *hostess*.

Monica had a dinner engagement with Keith for that evening, and though Sheila said indifferently, "Fine— bring him along," Monica decided against it. She wanted to see Sheila as the mistress of Edgemont, she wanted to examine that other Sheila, with no distractions.

* * *

The first surprise of the evening was that a man named Hen—Hennessey—a neighbor—of whom Monica had never before heard—was Sheila's partner for the occasion, her "date," so to speak; judging by his manner, his ease, his general high spirits, he was virtually cohosting the party with Sheila. "Monica dear, this is Hen," Sheila said in a bright false voice, drawing Monica forward as if she were a recalcitrant child, "—Hen is an old, old neighbor— I mean an old *friend*—old and dear, aren't you, Hen?— we've known each other for ages but we rarely *see* each other, it's a shame. Hen, Monica Jensen, Monica is a new friend—a very dear *new* friend—she's renting that place Morton and I used to own, that house, you know, on the Olcottsville Road, yes, the one the Dorrs lived in— Monica is teaching at the Academy, isn't that *interesting?* All those *adolescents*—"

Hennessey was tall, wide-shouldered, handsome in a slightly florid way; in his early fifties, perhaps. His handshake was strong, his smile gratifying. Within a few seconds he had muddled her name ("Mona?—ah yes: *Monica*") and mixed up the Glenkill Academy with another local school, the Quaker school in New Hope (*"That's* an excellent place too, my boy Josh went there"), but his gallantry toward Monica, as Sheila's friend, assuaged her feelings; and made her feel, for a while at least, that she had not made a mistake in coming.

And the other guests, the "horsey" set, the country squires and their wives—they too were extremely interesting; and certainly well-spoken. Like Hen they were warmly friendly with Monica, asking her questions, the same sort of questions ("Do you like it here," "How long have you been here," "How *is* the Academy—we hear such conflicting reports"), flattering her with their attention though (as Monica well knew) none of it could be sincere.

Hen made Monica a strong drink, which she accepted with gratitude; and as she sipped it, nervously, contemplatively, she decided it had been naive of her to be surprised that Sheila was on such companionable terms with a man she had never mentioned to her. Hen, Hennessey, an old dear friend and neighbor, with a five-hundred-acre farm off the New Egypt Pike; Hen, a man of considerable attractions; quite clearly wealthy. Perhaps the two were lovers, or had been lovers at one time: what of it?

No doubt there were many such men scattered through the world—lovers, former lovers, confidants, old dear friends—a network of people who had in common their connection, licit or otherwise, with Sheila Trask.

Am I envious, Monica wondered.

Am I going to be bitter, Monica wondered.

Then, closely watching Sheila and Hen together, noting the high gay insistent tone of Sheila's voice, and Hen's studied gallantry, his somewhat too affable flirtatious air, Monica decided that the relationship was only superficial.

Hen and Sheila, superficial.

Superficial if lovers; if "old dear friends."

Still, Monica was impressed by Sheila in her role of hostess: the mistress of Edgemont.

Of course the woman was under an incalculable strain —of course she had dosed herself with therapeutic drinks, beforehand—but her performance was controlled, polished—she gave little hint of unease—she *was* mistress of Edgemont after all, and quite looked the part.

Monica thought Sheila unnaturally beautiful, more beautiful indeed, than she'd ever seen her before. She wore a long dress of crimson crushed velvet in a wrap-over style that casually, but very casually, revealed a good deal of the luminous-pale skin of her chest; gold chains of varying degrees of weight and splendor were looped about her neck; gold earrings—not unlike Monica's silver Moroccan earrings—fell gracefully, in coils, to brush against her shoulders. Painting a face, Sheila once said, a face overlaid upon one's own, was a cheerful sort of challenge if one didn't take it seriously; she quite enjoyed the task, bringing to it her artist's penchant for stylish legerdemain, making of distinctly faded and flawed skin a ceramic-smooth surface—coloring in the lips brightly, slyly—applying with a tiny brush several shades of eye shadow (mauve, beige, dark brown)—shaping the brows so that they were not *quite* so savage but might be seen as exotic. Such beauty is sheer trumpery, Sheila said, therefore the sport of it, that, for a few giddy hours at least, one is what one seems: one "is" beautiful if one "seems" beautiful. And it was all very innocent, wasn't it?

Though thin, nearly gaunt, Sheila managed to suggest a lanky sort of luxuriance, with her springy black hair, her crushed velvet dress, the earrings, the gold chains, the rings on her fingers that flashed and glittered. (She had scrubbed her hands clean with turpentine that very morning and had done, to Monica's surprise, a creditable job.) She managed to suggest too a childlike gaiety, a virginal chasteness, even as she and Hen kept up their flirtatious banter, and, from time to time, swaying on her feet in imitation of drunkenness (for of course she *was* drunk) Sheila slipped an arm around his neck to steady herself.

When Sheila's gaze locked with hers Monica believed she could sense her friend's slight embarrassment—for this was all such a sham, wasn't it—a masquerade, a sustained deception—but in the next instant Sheila smiled, showing her teeth, and called out aggressively so that all her guests heard, *"Aren't* you lovely tonight, Monica—!"

"Don't tell me, please, that you're an artist too, like Sheila," the man seated beside Monica said, staring at her. "You could be an artist's model."

"Really?" said Monica, greatly amused. "What sort of artist?"

She was looking uncommonly good, she knew; and it did not hurt her prospects that she was the youngest woman seated at Sheila Trask's dining room table.

The man—his name was Win—"Winthrop"—smiled at her as if she'd said something witty, which perhaps she had.

Monica in her black muslin dress with the fringed hem, long sleeves, a sash tied tight to emphasize her narrow waist—Monica with gold studs in her earlobes and the Moroccan necklace heavy about her neck—looked rather more Bohemian than Sheila Trask herself; and behaved with nearly as much abandon. She wasn't drunk but she *was* high: and what of it? The unusual necklace elicited a good deal of admiration from Sheila's guests, and compliments Monica deflected in Sheila's direction. ("Tell *Sheila*," she said. "It was her gift to me.") She had brushed her hair until it gleamed; fastened it with a clip; and, inspired, feeling playful, she had pinned a small white orchid the size of a daisy above her left ear, bought that afternoon in Olcottsville. It did her spirit good, Monica had thought, regarding herself critically in her bedroom mirror, to look striking once in a while; to appear as that golden girl of old whose promise and whose good luck had so mysteriously drained away.

Win repeated his question more seriously—*was* Monica an artist?—how had she and Sheila become acquainted?—and Monica heard herself reply in a vague charming silken voice, for, suddenly, it seemed that she too was caught up in a flirtation. Win was clearly attracted to her; he was alone at the party (unmarried? divorced?); the wine she was drinking rushed wonderfully to her head. (To all the parts of her body, in fact. Warming and consoling. In such de-

ightful secrecy.) Win regarded her with such interest—
such flattering interest—it scarcely mattered what Monica
said, only the way in which she said it; the intonations she
gave to her voice, the smiles she smiled, the movements of
her eyes—the old trickery of flirtation, which she had forgotten. (Or was she simply out of practice, Monica wondered, amused.) Others at the table were talking of
horses—dear God, at such length, of horses!—and there
was a great deal of fuss over Sheila's paella (which Hen
graciously if almost too solemnly served, calling out the
ingredients as he spooned them onto plates: chicken,
shrimp, sausage, clams, squid: there seemed to be some
silly joke about the squid, which one of the women at the
table professed to fear); so Monica and Win were able to
speak together at some length, uninterrupted, about—but
what *had* they talked about, Monica wondered afterward
—and they were able to establish the fact that they liked
each other, they liked each other very much.

The man's name was Jackson Winthrop, Win to his
friends ("You're all Wins and Hens, aren't you?" Monica
said. "Is it a code?"); he owned a farm on the far side of
Olcottsville; he was in his late forties; divorced three years
before. He described himself with a self-congratulatory
sort of irony as a Bucks County gentleman farmer though
he no longer farmed and if he was gentle it was surely not
by choice. "Just genes, heredity, Anglican schools," he
said. With a meaty sigh, leaning close, he told Monica that
he was "your standard divorced man: embittered, impoverished, but still optimistic."

Monica decided not to tell him that she was a divorced
woman.

Most of their exchange would have struck Monica, by
day, and in the impartial light of sobriety, as insincere,
even dangerous. But, in Sheila's elegant dining room,

amidst tall candles and quivering flames and long-stemmed Venetian glasses and Monica's heightened sense of herself (she could see her blond image floating diaphanous and lovely, a ghost-beauty in a mirror above Sheila's antique Spanish sideboard) it all seemed highly significant; intriguing. And it was certainly flattering.

Win *was* attractive, Monica thought, though rather too self-assured, his smile too nudging, his manner overly familiar. He poured wine into Monica's glass, he leaned toward her, he brushed, by accident, surely, the back of his hand against her breast; his eyes were nearly lashless though alert, mirthful. How very unlike poor Keith Renwick, Monica thought. (She felt a stab of guilt; and some apprehension. When she telephoned Keith to break off their engagement for the evening—with the most feeble of excuses: Sheila Trask needed help out at Edgemont, her upcoming show, etc.—Keith had replied in short clipped sentences, and had not asked when he might see her again. I'm sorry, Monica told him, feeling, suddenly, truly sorry, but it was too late, perhaps; she had hurt him for the final time; she would not be hearing from him again.)

"I'm relieved that you aren't an artist like Sheila," Win said in a lowered voice. "It's so difficult to know what to make of her, isn't it!—they say she's very, very good— they say her paintings sell for a lot of money—but I just can't see it, you know—I mean I've *tried*—all of us around here have tried—but we just can't *see* it. Flaxman made more sense, I think—you could see he'd done a lot of work on his sculptures—but Sheila's things, Sheila's art, it's all so *mysterious*. Don't you think? What do *you* think? One night at this table Flaxman got into an argument with someone about Jackson Pollock—you know who he is, of course—all the squiggles and heavy looping strands of paint, raw paint—Flaxman said Pollock was one of the greatest artists of the twentieth century and one of his guests—I forget who, it *wasn't* me!—said 'Bullshit'—'Bullshit and I can prove it'—and things were pretty hot for a while, let me tell you."

Monica glanced up at Sheila, who was busily absorbed in a chafing dish, with Hen's help—the dessert was an exquisite soufflé au rhum—and took no notice of Monica's conversation. "Well—how did he prove it?" Monica asked.

"Prove what?" asked Win.

"He said: 'Bullshit and I can prove it,' and I'm wondering how he proved it," Monica said.

Win smiled at her, his cheeks creasing, dimpling. He must have thought she had said something especially witty because he made no reply at all.

At midnight Monica disappointed Win, and Sheila as well, by saying she had to leave.

Win immediately offered to drive her home but Monica, prepared, said she had her own car; she'd come to Edgemont under her own powers and she intended to return home under her own powers. "A point of honor," she said, winking.

"Please stay," Sheila said. "You can't mean to leave *now.*"

"I should have left an hour ago," Monica said. "I'm drunk."

"You aren't drunk—is she, Win?" Sheila cried, taking hold of Monica's arm. "And if you are, that's all the more reason not to drive home alone."

But Monica was adamant, Monica was on her way.

Sheila and Win both saw her to her car. Win shook hands with her, and Sheila surprised her by embracing her rather roughly, and kissing her on the mouth—this kiss, too, rough and hurried, scarcely affectionate.

"Then, if you insist, good night!" Sheila said in playful bitterness, adjusting the little orchid above Monica's ear.

Driving home, slowly, luxuriously, Monica kept her mind blank. She was awash, it seemed, in a remarkable erotic warmth; a pulsing erotic warmth; concentrated in her loins but radiating out, wonderfully out, to all parts of her body.

That night she dreamt of the most extraordinary painting, fluid, three-dimensional, throbbing with life: Sheila's painting, perhaps, but only partly imagined, still in the process of being transcribed. Monica was staring at the painting yet at the same time she was in it; swimming in its sweet radiant warmth, in its fleshy-sweet erotic warmth; scarcely daring to breathe because the sensation was so exquisite, so precarious, so forbidding.

And, ah!—if someone were to kiss her, harshly, impatiently, on the lips, what then—!

10

A TRIUMPH OF a party!—so Monica telephoned Sheila next day, to exclaim.

"Was it?" Sheila said indifferently.

She had no interest in talking about the party, evidently; she seemed to have very nearly forgotten it.

Before they broke off their conversation Sheila asked, suddenly, if Jack Winthrop had telephoned her yet. "No," Monica said. "He will," Sheila said, "—and if I were you, I wouldn't see him."

11

ARIADNE'S THREAD, THE secrets of the labyrinth, the convolutions of the human brain. . . .

The canvases were to be completed and taken away, by van, in twelve days. Monica was on the telephone a half-dozen times in a single morning, making arrangements; her throat was hoarse with arguing.

One Sunday an assistant from the Laurence James Gallery came out to Edgemont, to meet with Sheila; and Sheila insisted that Monica be present; she couldn't get through the visit by herself, she said. (The young man, thin, blond, nervously handsome, a chain-smoker as addicted as Sheila Trask herself, stayed and stayed and stayed . . . until there was nothing to do, Monica realized, but invite him to dinner: she would prepare something in Sheila's kitchen for the three of them.) Since the night of the party Sheila had lost a good deal of her spirit and energy. At Monica's insistence she was no longer taking drugs—she moved slowly, lethargically, with a sort of bodily irony that Monica thought unnerving.

(She isn't really sick, Monica told herself carefully. It's a stratagem of some kind, a way of making art.)

As to the paintings themselves—Monica saw them so often, so obsessively, even, it appeared, in her sleep, she no longer "saw" them at all. There was a distinct internal logic to the series which one began to feel but it would have been impossible for Monica to talk of it. To murmur that the canvases were beautiful—powerful—compelling —lyric—or "lyrically violent" (as the young man from the Laurence James Gallery said)—seemed quite beside the point. All that was significant about them was interior, secret, indefinable; they possessed their own integrity, they *were*. Monica began to understand her friend's almost fanatical interest in technique since "idea" could only be embodied by way of technique; Sheila detested the very notion of a conceptualist art—words were an admission of failure. So, in the studio, hour upon hour passed in absolute silence. It was a place where language did not determine action. It was a place, Monica sometimes thought, prior to language. To enter it—to dare to enter it—was to surrender the power of words, and to submit to another sort of power altogether.

The paintings were succeeding, however. They *were* beautiful in their own oblique intransigent way. Of that Monica felt morally certain.

"Yes, fine, but the thing is," the young blond man said, lighting up another of his cigarettes, and fixing Monica with a look—intimate, slightly reproachful—she didn't at all like, "—will she get them out of here on time? They're finished now but of course you can't tell her that—you dare not tell the woman *any*thing. Frankly, Monica, this is the worst I've seen Sheila in ages. We'd all been led to believe, you know, from talking to you on the phone, that you had things in control—I mean, my dear, a little *more* in control."

12

MONICA WAS BEGINNING to get sick, Monica felt at times a veering light-headed sensation as of unreality ... not that the world about her (walls, ceilings, floors, windows, students' attentive faces) was unreal but that she herself, passing uncertainly through it, was unreal.

She had missed a few classes this spring. Nothing extraordinary—just a few classes.

She was forced to miss ("unavoidably") one or another meeting—a general faculty meeting, an English Department curriculum meeting—since she was needed elsewhere. Of course she made her excuses; she was careful to make her excuses; and to be sincerely sorry, *sorry*.

And if she slipped away from her office in the afternoon—her office hours being 4:00–5:00—with a note taped to the door canceling her conferences for the day—if she hurried across the lush greening lawn (bordered by tulips, daffodils, jonquils set fastidiously in place) to get to her car, and to freedom, escape—for she was needed, badly needed, at Edgemont: the knowledge weighed upon her obsessively—if she disappointed a boy or two, or three: surely they would not be vindictive, and complain of her to her chairman?—for after all they liked her, they admired her, she was reasonably certain of that.

"I will make up for it," Monica thought, "—after the show opens. Once the show opens. Then—"

Sheila was saying in a small flat voice that she couldn't allow the canvases out of the studio. Not that she was thinking of destroying them but it was clear to her now that she had months of work before her: the show would be premature: she would be exposed: her life would be over.

"I made a miscalculation," Sheila said. "Going to North Africa when I did." She paused; she stared hard at Monica, quite clearly hating her. "Going to North Africa when I did, because of you. And my head was prized off. Too much light—external light. External fucking light when that has nothing to do with anything *here*."

Monica was stung by these words, yet, oddly, not very surprised. She was losing her capacity to be surprised: as drained of energy, in truth, as Sheila Trask herself, and not nearly so strong.

Monica said calmly, even briskly, that the arrangements with the gallery were all made. The van; the driver; the invitations; the plans for the champagne reception and the dinner afterward; the small press conference. ("Don't worry, I'll be with you," Monica said, "I've promised, and I will.")

Sheila seemed to be listening, yet, a minute later, she repeated that the paintings weren't ready to be hung. If Morton were here he would know: he'd give his judgment and that would be that. He never humored her, Sheila said. She was sitting slouched on the edge of a windowsill, beneath what seemed very nearly a blast of warm white humid sunshine, unflattering to her sallow skin, her pouched eyes. She dragged a hand slowly across her mouth. *He* never exploited or manipulated her, she said. Again she looked hard at Monica, her mouth twisting as if she were about to cry; or utter a violent epithet.

"No one is exploiting or manipulating you," Monica said carefully. "You know that."

"Do I? Do I? What do I *know!*—only what you fuckers tell me," Sheila said.

"Sheila, you don't mean that," Monica said, going to lay a hand lightly on Sheila's shoulder. She would quiet her, Monica thought, she would stroke her into submission, as one might a frightened child or an animal.

But Sheila slapped her hand away. "Don't *touch* me!" she said.

Monica will long remember:

In the Founders Room at the Glenkill Academy—enormous fieldstone fireplace, bay windows of leaded glass, walnut paneling on the walls, comfortably weathered Oriental carpets—in a place of brown leather couches, also comfortably weathered, and folding chairs, and spring flowers in clay vases spaced about the room—in the late, late afternoon of a rainy May day—one of Monica's interminable days—a day so very long, so very convoluted and ambagious, she could not have said, in her state of dazed exhaustion, when it began, or how, or why—in this place (but why *is* she here?) Monica sits listening to boys between the ages of fifteen and seventeen reading their "recent work" (poetry, prose, other). The audience consists of thirty-six boys (Monica has counted them) and a scattering of faculty members (eight at first, but now two or three have slipped away) and of course the chaplain's wife, Jill Starkie: Jill in a bright blue velour smock over blue jeans, Jill seated on the floor in front of the fireplace, hugging her knees, her head turned to one side in an attitude of intense ecstatic concentration.

A boy is reading a poem about death, and rain strikes in spirited little waves against the windows, and Monica *is* listening, Miss Jensen *is* listening, her own expression alertly attentive, her eyes glazing over with teacherly sympathy. (Most of the boys reading this afternoon are from her classes.) Absentmindedly she strokes the scar on her jaw, that secret pattern of striations in the flesh, hers, *her*. She concentrates on the boy and his poem but cannot hear the words because she is hearing other words, I hate you, I want to die, I loathe and despise you and I want to die, and her own voice lifting, shrill with weariness and despair, but which words had she uttered?—she could not now recall. Perhaps she said nothing, perhaps she has imagined everything.

When the reading is over she will hurry to telephone Sheila.

Unless—granted the distinct possibility of the phone simply ringing and ringing and ringing out there—it would be wisest for her simply to get in her car and drive to Edgemont.

Now a boy, one of Monica's most earnest students, is reading a prose poem, as he calls it, a "cubist collage" as he calls it, consisting of fragments of hallucinatory dialogue and description; and Monica tries to listen; and Monica tries very hard to care. The boy is someone of whom she has grown fond this past semester, one of the students who clearly admires her; perhaps, if it comes to it *(will* it?) such students will make a difference in her career at Glenkill. For Monica is not teaching quite so well as she once was, and Monica is not quite so . . . interested, it seems, in the school and its activities ("I was hurt, Monica, yes I was truly hurt, and I think I should tell you!—I *was* hurt," Jill Starkie said a few days ago, cornering Monica in the library, "—you know you distinctly *promised* to drop by and James hurried back from Philadelphia just for the occasion—"). When she is present, however, as she is now (5:40 P.M. of this long long day) she gives every appearance of being intensely interested, doesn't she; sympathetic; devoted.

Monica notes the curious phenomenon that when daffodils pass their prime their petals become paper-thin. The colorful centers remain (yellow, orangish-yellow) but the outer petals turn transparent.

Monica notes that the majority of boys in the Founders

Room, scattered about on the sofas, the folding chairs, and the carpets, are dressed in the latest preppie fashion: school ties, of course; and white shirts; here and there a school blazer; but they are wearing shoes (loafers, jogging shoes) without socks—as they have been all winter, no matter the freezing temperatures.

("Don't your heels get raw, without socks?" Monica asked them, amused, genuinely curious. "Doesn't your skin chafe, and bleed?" The boys allowed her to know that such considerations did not matter at all to them—that Miss Jensen simply did not, could not, understand. If shoes are to be worn without socks then shoes are to be worn without socks no matter the discomfort.)

Monica notes, waking from her trance, a sudden restlessness in the room; a flurry of whispers; muffled laughter. The boy solemnly intoning the cubist collage has made an error . . . a blunder of taste, or discretion . . . he has spiced his nearly indecipherable presentation with such disturbing words as *vomit, entrails, semen, love* . . . and it seems to be (*can* it be?) that his prose poem is a homosexual fantasy, a lyric celebrating "gayness." . . . Monica, frightened, wants to lean over to him, to command him to stop: doesn't he know how he is exposing himself, and in this intolerant company: doesn't he know how the other boys, now listening closely, are smirking, staring, grinning in incredulous contempt. . . .

But she cannot stop him, of course; and, in any case, he comes to an end a few minutes later; and there is a very faint round of applause—*very* faint, which he nonetheless acknowledges with a defiant little smile.

Brian Farley stops Monica, as she knew he would, to say that she really should have checked with the boys in her classes, to see what they intended to read. "Leonard isn't a very stable person, as you must know," Farley said, "and this afternoon's performance isn't going to do him any good."

Monica knows that Farley is right; but her pulses leap in a fiery little rush of irritation. She says stubbornly that she couldn't possibly have checked out her students' material —she couldn't possibly have censored any of it.

And suddenly they are arguing, in the corridor outside the Founders Room.

"Your colleagues took time to glance through their students' material, and no one 'censored' anything," Farley says. "It was only a matter of good taste and judgment."

"Our students aren't children," Monica says, "—they can hardly be told what to do. Leonard thinks of himself as a writer—he's very serious about everything he does—I don't see how I—"

"Never mind about Leonard," Farley says angrily. "The fact is that while our students aren't children they aren't adults either, they're adolescents, some of them are extremely immature, they look to us for adult supervision which is the point, isn't it," he says, as Monica begins to draw away, her face stiff with opposition, "—the point of the school? Of people like us?"

Monica's rage carries her for some distance, for some miles, until, suddenly, braking her car to a stop on the Poor Farm Road, she feels a wave of dizziness, vertigo—a sense that the world is too vivid and solid and hard-edged to contain her.

The panic attack lasts for approximately ten minutes.

And when, finally—slowly—it lifts she finds herself drenched in perspiration; chilled and shivering. She cannot remember at first where she was coming from or where, with such a sense of desperate urgency, she is headed.

13

Sheila telephoned to apologize, hours later.

Hours later, Sheila telephoned to say she'd been off her head, she hadn't known what she said or what she meant, she hoped Monica would forgive her.

(But what *had* she said? She couldn't remember.)

She was wretchedly lonely, she said.

She said she would continue with the plans, the arrangements, if Monica thought that wise.

She said it would be over with soon.

She said that her basic wish was simply to die and get the entire business finished but (this in a voice trembling with hilarity) she was balked by the thought of a memorial service of some kind . . . rows of solemn "mourners" . . . sappy banalities that were sure to be said aloud and perhaps even published.

Finally, after a pause, Monica spoke.

She said, gripping the receiver tight, that she very much doubted that Sheila wanted to be *dead*. "Think of how dull it would be," she added.

Sheila agreed. But the problem was how to get through the next hour, the next half-hour, the next five minutes. "If I can manage that I can manage anything," she said slowly. "One breath and then another and then another. . . ."

"Yes," said Monica. "One breath and then another."

"And once the show is over . . ."

"Yes."

"Then, then . . ."

"Yes."

"Then I'll be free," Sheila said. "And I'll make it up to

you, all you've endured for my sake." She paused; Monica could hear her harsh quickened breathing. "I'll be able to love you then," she said. "I can't love anyone now. But then . . . If you don't betray me . . ."

14

MONICA TOOK AN entire day off from school—her excuse
being, quite legitimately, she thought, a sick friend—a
friend who needed help—and drove Sheila to Philadelphia, to her doctor; but, as Monica was parking her car,
Sheila informed her suddenly that she couldn't see the
man; she wouldn't see him. He would only tell tales about
her, making out that she was sicker than she was, and, in
any case, she *wasn't* sick: she felt fine.

So they sat in the car and quarreled.

Ten minutes. Fifteen. And Monica's voice shook, and
Monica began to cry, and Monica screamed at her, finally,
why hadn't she thought of any of this before, back home.

". . . I wanted to please you, Monica," Sheila said softly.
"I know you're angry with me and I wanted to please you,
it was all for *you.*"

Monica made an appointment with a young doctor in Edgarsville whom someone at school recommended highly,
but, this time, she was shrewd enough to make the appointment without telling Sheila. And, promptly at 9:00 in
the morning she arrived at Sheila's studio to tell her that
she was scheduled to see a doctor at 10:00 so would she
please get ready, they were leaving immediately. Sheila
protested feebly, but acquiesced. And this time she actually
saw the doctor: Monica waited a good forty-five minutes
while she was examined: and when she finally emerged she
was smiling, reproachful, triumphant: she told Monica that
it was as she'd expected all along, she was in exemplary
health.

"Don't you have to go to a hospital for tests?—for a blood test, at least?" Monica asked doubtfully.

"Not at all," Sheila said. "My blood is fine."

"You're sure—?"

"My blood is fine and *I* am fine," Sheila said.

Driving fast along the curving country roads, her head ringing, her eyes glazed over with fatigue, Monica thought suddenly: Both of us might die.

The logic (radiantly simple, blinding as a sunburst) was that: if one of them died the other would survive and everything would be thrown off balance. But if they both died equilibrium would be reestablished.

15

MONICA LIKED TO think *without warning,* as the cliché would have it, but no doubt she had warning, she had warnings, which she chose to ignore.

His face an immense creased moon, his eyes bright with hatred.

The veins in his forehead standing out.

Furious red worms, those veins; pulsing; giving off heat.

". . . So why the hell did you come up here, then," he said, the heel of his hand striking her bare shoulder, his voice incredulous, mocking, meant perhaps to be light, ". . . a big girl like you. A big growed-up girl like you."

Later he said, crouched over her: "I know you're judging me, how can I do anything if you're judging me. . . ."

Monica's lips were so bruised, so numbed, she couldn't answer.

She might have apologized but she couldn't answer.

The ruddy dimpled flesh, the ridges of fat quivering at waist and thighs and belly. Monica had misplaced his name, a nickname; a fond sweet chummy name. And he seemed in the exigencies of his travail to have forgotten hers. He murmured, "Oh honey, Jesus . . . honey . . . you sweet cunt . . . you sweet, sweet . . ."

A bedside clock was ticking loud and fast.

Monica thought: He won't strangle me, he isn't the sort.

Monica thought: His name is either Win or Hen, it's all a code.

She tried not to cry out with the pain but at last she did, it simply wasn't to be prevented, she was in terror sud-

214

denly that her insides had never healed (the abortion, the scooping out, the menstrual periods that had lasted for ten, eleven days) and that she would begin hemorrhaging. He was now grinding his mouth against hers, teeth bared against her teeth, a grin of sorts, he was saying, "Why did you come up here if . . . You bitch . . ." parting her lips, bruising them. Monica tasted blood but (perhaps) it was only her imagination. So much is imagined, so much is mere hysteria. Hen, Win. Win, Hen. Though the silly drunken golden girl meant only to accommodate and certainly did not resist, her lover was impatient nonetheless, keenly disappointed nonetheless, and bent upon exacting punishment. And there was his tongue, grown immense, poking. His gigantic tongue. And his not-quite-erect penis grinding against her.

The clock ticked, Monica went limp, an old strategy, an old wifely habit. She was thinking of Ariadne's thread. You took hold of it, you trusted to it, and then it snapped in your fingers. . . . She was thinking of something dreamy and fluid, an element through which one had to thrust oneself, with great effort. The danger of suffocation, of a heart stopping in midbeat. . . .

She was sobbing helplessly, shamelessly. It was all over but she couldn't stop sobbing.

Her breasts, her nipples, had been sucked and bitten until they bled. The insides of her thighs were raw. He'd done something, hadn't he, with his fingers, his nails, she *was* bleeding but dear God what did it matter, it was all over, he hadn't meant (he said) to be rough, he hadn't meant to get carried away, why hadn't she told him if he was hurting her.

"Jesus," he said, staring, "—a big growed-up girl like you, a friend of Sheila Trask's—"

16

SHEILA CRADLED HER head, rocked her, asked if she wanted to be taken to a doctor. If she wanted Sheila to report that bastard to the police.

Because he'd forced her, after all. Technically and legally it was rape.

Monica started laughing, then Monica was crying again, huddled in Sheila's arms.

No she didn't want to be taken to a doctor and no she didn't want to report Win to the police it was her own fault primarily, just let it go.

Sheila held her; rocked her; lit a cigarette, blowing the smoke over Monica's head, stroking her hair, murmuring, telling her she should never have consented to see Jack Winthrop—*she* should never have introduced them—it had all been a bloody mistake. If Monica had only—

Monica drew away from her, stiffening in opposition. She whispered that Sheila could go home whenever she wished; the emergency, such as it was, was over; all she wanted to do was sleep.

"If you're sure you will be all right," Sheila said uncertainly. "If you don't want a doctor. . . ."

"No thank you, Sheila," Monica said. "I think you've done enough."

17

THE DAY OF Sheila Trask's opening was a Wednesday, the champagne reception began at 5:30 P.M., but Monica made her excuses and stayed away; Monica was teaching her classes.

And afterward she sat in her empty classroom, staring into space.

She knew she was sick but she didn't know the degree to which it was commonplace, a matter of spring flu, the usual malaise, passed from student to student and among the faculty members. One big happy family at Glenkill, James Starkie had joked, months ago, which means too, he said, winking, we pass our diseases around, and Monica and another of the guests (his face and name long forgotten) exchanged a startled amused glance. The unintentional wit of James Starkie's remark passed otherwise unnoticed: it was a noisy festive evening at the chaplain's house, fragrant with Jill Starkie's Chanel No. 5 and the smell of too-sweet sherry. New York State wine, James Starkie said, as if the fact were noteworthy. Monica remembered how James had kissed her: how suddenly, how impulsively: that good-natured comradely kiss that threatened nothing and had not given pain. Now the Starkies disliked her. Their smiles were strained, their greetings subdued. She had disappointed them by failing to do something or other and then by failing a second time, she had hurt Jill, perhaps she had irrevocably offended Jill, but should a Christian woman be so easily offended. . . .

Monica looked up dry-eyed to see one of her fifth-form boys standing in the doorway. Clearly embarrassed, his voice slightly trembling, he asked if anything was wrong. "Some of us were wondering, you know, if, well, you didn't leave after class and now it's pretty late and we were wondering if . . . if anything is wrong," the boy said. He was not one of Monica's very best students but he was a reliable A— student, helpful in class, sweet-tempered, attractive. He wants me to break down in front of him, Monica thought, they are all waiting for that. So she said quietly: "No. Nothing is wrong. Please close the door when you leave."

18

THE TELEPHONE RANG and rang, and finally Monica answered it, her mouth stale from sleep. Sheila was speaking —Sheila was speaking excitedly—and Monica tried to make sense of her words—such a buzz, such a flurry!—and such pretense ("Monica, why the hell *aren't* you here, don't understand")—and after a while, after many minutes, Monica interrupted to say she couldn't talk on the phone any longer: she was going back to bed.

Calmer now, Sheila thanked her for the flowers—a dozen long-stemmed red roses; but Christ did she *miss* her! The opening had gone well enough, considering. Sheila had held up well enough, considering. But there were such marvelous people Sheila would have liked Monica to meet, old friends of hers, a handful of younger artists as well, one of them, a kid named Peck, a fantastic talent—

Monica repeated that she was going back to bed. When Sheila gave no reply she simply hung up the receiver; and the remainder of the night passed undisturbed.

19

NOW MY PUNISHMENT has begun, Monica thought.

She lay shivering and sweating in her bed. She was
unable to sleep—her head ached, her stomach cramped
violently—yet suddenly it seemed she was being wakened
by a fierce wintry wind, and rain slashing against the windows. In the morning, dragging herself from her bed, she
saw that most of the blossoms in her crab apple trees—
four comely little trees, beautiful fleshy-pink flowers—had
been blown off during the night.

They telephoned her from school, solicitous, prying.

She told them in a calm distinct voice that, at the moment, she wasn't feeling well. But she would certainly be
back the next day; she intended to meet her 8:00 class as
usual. Surely, she said, she was guilty of no great criminal
neglect.

Lying back, she felt Win's heartbeat—she remembered
it, suddenly, an angry pumping that communicated itself to
her own body. As if his heart, at that critical instant, were
hers; in the cavity of her chest where her own heart might
have been.

Monica regretted one thing: that, since coming to teach at
the Glenkill Academy, she had always been too busy to
explore the boxwood maze behind the headmaster's residence.

If the garden had been between her building and her
parking lot no doubt she would have strolled in it from
time to time, but it was rather out of the way, she seemed
always to be in a hurry, her hair flying in the wind. Now

she was pleasantly surprised to find herself in the garden, alone, unobserved, able to walk where she wished, and at her own pace; while at the same time she remained lying in her damp sheets, eyes gummed shut.

The maze consisted of boxwood and English ivy and laurels with fine glossy leaves. Monica stared, Monica wandered. She was not yet lost. She had always understood that the sprayed and sculpted forms, the odorless blossoms, the narrow graveled walks of tiny pink pebbles and oyster chips were a testament to the school's affluence and good taste, its Anglophile tradition. At the center of the maze was a small fountain where two slender stone figures—a faun and a nymph—cavorted forever in the bright sparkling water.

Monica began to walk more quickly. She was frightened, exhilarated. She could not be truly lost because this was only (wasn't it?) the headmaster's garden, a small contained space. And surely she was being observed after all. The Glenkill faculty, the Glenkill students. Her own students of whom she had grown very fond, in her warm inattentive way. They would not allow her to injure herself, they would not jeer at her, standing apart from her predicament. Poor Monica: poor Miss Jensen: only partly clothed, smelling of bed and sweat and vomit, wandering sobbing and lost in the boxwood maze. . . .

Leave me alone, Monica whispered. Let me die.

20

AFTER SHEILA'S OPENING at the Laurence James Gallery a good deal happened, and it happened quickly.

For one thing, the show was considered a success. Even (in the words of one of the gallery assistants, with whom Monica spoke on the phone) a "great success."

One of the well-to-do collectors who had bought Flaxman's work was now interested in acquiring major pieces by Sheila Trask; which fact, not kept entirely confidential, had the agreeable result of triggering "interest" among other collectors. And there were representatives of private galleries, and of the Museum of Modern Art, and the Whitney, and the Guggenheim, and . . .

But Sheila seemed scarcely to be interested. She told Monica that her show was a success because the paintings obviously hadn't been priced high enough: if they had been, perhaps none would have sold.

Sheila was agreeing to do interviews and then canceling them at the last minute. It took four hours for her to be photographed for a feature in *Vogue*—the woman was so restless, so euphoric, she simply couldn't sit still. Her very hair crackled about her face as if with electricity but she wasn't thinking of her show, her success, the sudden attention being paid to her, she was thinking of a new project, her next project.

Day and night were queerly and wonderfully commingled, as ideas, impressions, images bombarded her. She was dreaming, she said, with her eyes open: could anything be more exquisite! These were visual ideas, contentless forms, motion, wave-motion, hairline fractures as of (for instance) great blocks of ice, fractures radiating in several directions at once, perhaps even in several dimensions ("Is time a dimension?" Sheila asked) at once. Ah, it was nothing she could explain! Nothing that made any sense!

She wanted, she said suddenly, to fly to South America in a few weeks. From there she would go by boat to Antarctica: but she intended to go alone.

Well—as it developed, perhaps not *entirely* alone.

For there was the matter suddenly of Peck.

Twenty-five-year-old Peck who came out to Edgemont for a few days, Peck who was tall, very lean, lanky, silent, appearing sullen though in truth (as Sheila insisted) he was quite good-natured, once you came to know him. By coincidence Peck shared Sheila's interest in Antarctica. In Peck it was very nearly an obsession, he wanted to paint and paint and paint ice floes, ice mountains, air scintillating with vapor, he knew what he wanted but (as Sheila said) he wasn't in a financial position to get what he wanted, not yet. He'd had several group exhibits, two one-man shows, SoHo primarily, his things had sold modestly and had been well reviewed, though not widely reviewed, he was at the very start of what Sheila knew to be an extraordinary career, he quite astonished her with his eye, his painterly wit, a certain clairvoyance.

. . . Peck is the real thing, Sheila said, her eyes narrowed in an odd rapturous resentful way, he's just a kid and he's the real thing. Shit!

Sheila invited Monica over to Edgemont to meet this prodigy but Monica begged off: she was unwell: she was preoccupied. (Also, as she did not wish to tell Sheila, she looked frankly sick; she wouldn't have wanted anyone, especially Sheila, to see her in such a state.) Sheila went on at some length about her young artist friend, who, as it turned out, greatly admired *her* work . . . felt temperamen-

tally drawn to it . . . though ("Queer, isn't it!") he said that
Flaxman's work generally left him cold. In company,
Sheila said, Peck could sit silent and glowering for hours,
but when they were alone he talked wonderfully, beautifully, for a young man with no consistent schooling he
knew so much, far more, Sheila said, than she'd known at
that age: Monica must meet him. ("Must I?" Monica said
faintly, ironically.) Though Sheila disapproved of representational art on principle she was overwhelmed, she said,
with a series of paintings Peck had done just last winter;
she'd bought two of them, in fact, would be hanging them
in her studio, Monica could see, of course the paintings
were not strictly representational—nothing hard-edged
about them, nothing photographic—they suggested dream
states, perhaps—large undefined spaces in which doors
were ajar, opened to various degrees, so that you could see
through one door to a shadowy interior where another door,
caught at a slant, was open—and so on, and so forth—and
there were windows too, seen at odd oblique angles—but
it wasn't so clear as Sheila was making out, the effect of
the paintings was altogether different—"Of course what
interests him is problem solving in terms of space, open
areas and closed, you'd see, Monica, you will see, when
you come over."

In the end Sheila brought Peck to Monica's house uninvited, they could only stay for a few minutes, she said,
they were on their way elsewhere, she was euphoric, handsome, rather loud, too restless to sit down while Peck,
hardly troubling to say hello to Monica, or to look at her,
sprawled lazily on the sofa, his long legs spread and his
arms limp, slung over the cushions. He looked precisely
his age, twenty-five; he was unshaven, sullen; clearly
bored; yet irritably attentive to Sheila Trask, who paced
about, talking rather too animatedly, swallowing large
mouthfuls of her drink, informing Monica of the fact that

he and she were having the most remarkable joint experience.... Each had dreams of gigantic ice islands, extinct volcanoes, dry valleys of volcanic ash...night skies glaring with pinpoints of intense light...each had dreams of blazing sunshine on snow...and when they spoke of these dreams each knew immediately what the other meant...as if they'd had the identical dreams at the identical times.

Solitude, and silence, and the fact that, there in Antarctica, "history" had not yet begun.

When are you leaving, Monica wanted to ask.

21

Now she was sick, seriously sick, but there was nothing to be done except wait it out.

Time leapt, pleated. Now sunshine dazed her and fell in lurid bright patches on the wall; now it was dusk; night; and someone was prowling about downstairs. She heard the clatter of horses' hooves. In the front hall? In her house? But Sheila would not dare, even as a jest . . . !

She saw Peck sprawled on her sofa, frowning, watching Sheila Trask closely, jealously; she felt the agitated movements of his eyeballs, which were her own. On the way out he and Sheila had passed through Monica's kitchen without noticing the stained glass lily balanced in one of the windows but Monica was not hurt, Monica did not care, she squirmed in dread only at the thought of how Peck passed judgment on her, what he said·afterward of her if he said anything at all.

A disfiguring scar, sensitive to the touch as an open wound, repulsive to look upon. As if Monica's legs were spread wide. As if the wound there were exposed. Good-bye! good-bye! Sheila cried in her great glaring joy, backing away. Good-bye!

Monica thought: I am to blame.

Monica thought: I am to blame so it is proper that I suffer, and soil the sheets.

She would be a stoic about this humiliating sickness (virulent intestinal flu, headache, fever, "unreality") because she knew she would not die. One does not die for a trifle after all. One does not die simply because one deserves to die.

Falling asleep, falling sick. *Falling*.

Falling in love: *falling*.

Once or twice, making her way downstairs, Monica nearly fell because of weakness; because her heart pumped too little oxygen (or too much) to her brain. This too is *falling*, she thought. This too must be acknowledged.

She took hold of the backs of chairs, door frames, the kitchen counter, making her slow staggering way, not quite remembering where she was headed—the refrigerator?—food?—but dear God, the very thought of it!—she would vomit everything up in the kitchen sink, she wouldn't even make it to the toilet.

Falling into bed, falling into sleep.

Falling.

She wondered mildly if she might fall too far—the notion of *falling* quite dazzled her—and never return.

Might one fall into the depths of one's own body, retreating to a small snug well-lit place deep in the brain, huddled there, knotted up, perfectly at ease, paralyzed, if you will, but perfectly at ease?—a languorous deathly sleep, the most delicious of sleeps?

What must be avoided, Monica thought, opening her burning eyes as the telephone rang, is self-pity.

So she didn't dare answer the phone. Wouldn't have dared, even if she could make it to the phone. For in her current state it was impossible to keep a note of self-pity out of her voice. For in her current state she cared for only one telephone call, one voice, which of course—being no fool, even with a temperature of 103°—she knew she would not hear.

Her hair, she discovered, had become coarse and greasy.

Her golden hair, so much admired!—but when she washed it, last time she washed it, how long was *that,* she had been frightened that so many hairs came out, sticking to her breasts, her belly, her legs, caught in the shower drain, a sickening sight. Perhaps it was a revelation but she needed no revelations, her fever darted and leapt and played about the ceiling, dazzled the insides of her eyelids, she had enough of revelations. Hairs in the shower and in the sink: Harold's, discovered by chance: and she had cleaned them out, deftly, not thinking a great deal about it, that was simply something she'd done, she was always to be observed doing something after all, every minute of every hour of every year, why not clean a husband's hairs out of a sink, the marriage would not last forever.

Had she the energy she might have turned Sheila's watercolor to the wall, or tossed it into the closet, or under the bed. Had she the energy she might have turned her mirrors to the wall, to spare herself their special revelation. It was particularly unnerving to see herself in the cabinet mirror in the bathroom—that sallow ravaged face, those puffed eyes, a dull-normal glaze over all—she, the golden girl!—now staggering and puking and damned grateful to have a place, a private place, in which to puke out her guts: which was the point, the sole point, wasn't it.

22

IN THAT BATHROOM, in the medicine cabinet, on the lower-most shelf amidst a stained toothbrush, and a tweezers, and a cuticle scissors, there is Monica's safety razor lying flat on a bit of dirty Kleenex.

Which vision never fails to bring a rush of tears to her eyes, for reasons she could not have named.

Which vision never fails to make her pulses leap, in a delirium of relief and expectation.

23

ON THE DAY of her thirtieth birthday Monica was clever enough to telephone home before her parents telephoned her, and she spoke cheerily enough, if at times rather faintly; so that was accomplished. Yes, she heard herself say, oh yes surely, yes of *course,* yes, *yes,* only a few more weeks now, sometime in mid-June I think, and there are examinations, there is commencement, I think I'm required to attend, yes of course, very well, *very* well, I've been extraordinarily lucky. So that was accomplished and she hadn't broken down and cried, it was far too late for tears, they would only be shocked and embarrassed.

Her nightgowns all stank but what could she do?—she hadn't the energy to wash them.

She slept in her underwear, or naked.

How odd: she was naked, yet the real estate agent took no notice, Mrs. Connor, Betty Connor as she'd introduced herself, shaking hands briskly, one professional woman to another, cards on the table, everything frank, crystal clear, yet, as Monica understood she *was* a fool to take on the responsibility of a house of this size. You'll be living alone? Betty Connor asked. Alone? One eyebrow lifted and quizzical, one side of her mouth raised.

Naked too, pleading with one of the men at school. Farley, it was. Farley, subtly altered. He spoke contemptuously to Monica without looking at her. (Of what sexual interest is a skeletal woman, a woman whose eyes have sunk back into her head . . .?) Monica was begging him in her dream as she had not begged him in real life to allow her to return to work but Farley knew her too well, he knew the secret in her heart, the sly terrible truth, that she did not care about him, she did not care, really, about her work, she cared about only one thing, one person, and if that were lost to her why should she care even about life? living? drawing one breath after another?

In fact she had tried to speak with Farley at the outset of her illness, some days before. But he happened never to be in his office and she found herself rerouted to one of the administrative assistants whose cold small smug voice maddened her. Miss Jensen this and Miss Jensen that, a just perceptible edge of disdain, mockery, contempt. She meant only to explain that she wouldn't be in to teach that day but she surely would be in to teach the following day without fail. But the conversation went poorly; she slammed down the receiver.

Another time when she telephoned the school she was told that her classes had been taken over for the remainder of the semester by one of her colleagues. Yes all the arrangements had been made. Yes the decision was irrevocable. Monica asked who the colleague was and was told————: a name she recognized but forgot immediately, as if this conversation were occurring in a dream and nothing could be retained. Licking her parched lips, swallowing, trying to clear her head Monica heard herself apologize . . . heard herself accuse Farley of deception, prejudice . . . heard herself pleading for another chance. She could get there, she promised, for her afternoon classes. For the next morning's classes at least.)

At any rate the birthday came and went without incident and now she was in her thirty-first year and would surely survive.

Monica is a good sport, she overheard.

She was grateful for the blinding headaches and the

sharp stabbing coiling pain in her bowels that signaled yet another attack of diarrhea: these sensations meant after all that she existed; she still lived; she had not yet melted into the surrounding air. (And the air hurt, chafed her delicate skin. There was an element of rapacity to it, as if it were greedy to devour her, to penetrate her and carry her off.) After the abortion she had spent days, perhaps it was weeks, months?—in a twilit state, feeling very little, caring about very little, examining the blood-soaked sanitary pads as if they were evidence of another's folly and not her own. Then, she had been numbed by drugs as well as by the trickery of her own mind, but now her punishment was her own, it inhabited every cubit of her flesh, and must be borne bravely.

There were rumors, whisperings, that Sheila Trask was going away again; and not alone.

Yet Monica was driving Sheila along the Poor Farm Road in Sheila's rattling station wagon and nothing seemed to be wrong. A blindingly bright day. Snow banked up high in the ditches. Monica did not dare glance up toward the sky but she felt its pressure, a cold hard ceramic blue like the blue of the tiles in Sheila's kitchen. The women were speaking softly together . . . laughing . . . Monica couldn't hear what they said but she understood their mood . . . and she understood that Sheila was joking when she reached out to take hold of the steering wheel and give it a sharp little twist. Monica was in control after all; Monica was supremely in control; it could do no harm, if Sheila teased.

The heavy car began to slip and slide and skid along the road. Monica tried to wrench the wheel away from Sheila's strong fingers, she pressed hard on the accelerator, suppose I call your bluff, Sheila, she whispered, but both women were laughing, both were enjoying themselves immensely, what danger in such sport? such childlike play? Monica gripped the wheel tight and Sheila tugged at it and the road dissolved into a blinding wall of light and both the women were laughing, convulsed in laughter.

24

Ten days, two weeks, and Monica began to recover.

It was late May and deceptively warm, in the afternoons in particular. One might be tempted to wander outside. To poke about in the old barns, to lie in the wet lush grass, to wander in the fields. It would be a humid spring, a balmy lilac-rich spring: the season of suicide: of raking over old humiliations and regrets like rotted matter in a compost heap.

The diarrhea was chronic but since she ate and drank very little she suffered less. Her stomach had shrunk to the size of (perhaps) a walnut. Her head was hollow, buzzing with static electricity, but the pain had subsided: now it was simply a matter of waiting.

Even at her sickest she had known the importance of not allowing anyone to guess what had happened. This sudden astonishing weakness, this exposure of her condition. The scar, the female gash, quivering nerve ends, repulsive to contemplate. She would be patient, she would not give in to the ignominy of terror. (When the roach had fallen into her hair, for instance. When everyone including Sheila had shrieked with laughter.)

She lay down, and was too weak to raise her head again, for hours, for hours. Still!—the blessed peace, the calm. She held herself tremblingly erect and opened the door of the medicine cabinet and saw, there, on the lowermost shelf, the razor, the packet of razor blades, the existing consolation. (What had Sheila told her once? . . . she'd visited a morgue, a dissection laboratory, she had forced herself to look at the bodies, she had forced herself to listen to the jokey medical students, the first incision is the only difficult task, Sheila was told, after that it's business as usual, after that you get completely caught up in technique, but the first incision *is* difficult, you'd better believe it, would you like to watch . . . ?)

Monica shook herself out of her doze, Monica thought about going outside again, risking the fresh air. If she raked over anything surely it should be a literal compost heap; in that direction, surely, lay health.

But she was too weak, suddenly. She wasn't going to make it after all.

25

MONICA HAD BEEN mistaken, she wasn't recovering, she was getting sicker, rapidly, deliriously. It intrigued her to think that her bones would soon poke through her skin—pelvic bones, collarbone, ribs. It intrigued her to think that that protective envelope of skin, her skin, might soon dissolve; and all of the world would rush in.

Now she might have telephoned for help but she was too weak.

A call placed to the Jensens in Wrightsville, Indiana—but she was too weak.

Too weak also to defend herself against Sheila Trask: Sheila towering over her: forcing her way into Monica's solitude where she wasn't wanted.

For, suddenly, Sheila was here; and the very air quaked.

For, suddenly, Sheila was running up the stairs, shouting Monica's name, frightened, angry, banging into the room. Monica, Monica for Christ's sake!—what have you done!—she sat heavily on the edge of the bed, her weight was a shock, her hand on Monica's forehead unnervingly cold. *"Are* you sick?" Sheila cried. "You are, you are!—oh God," staring at Monica incredulously, "—how could you have done this to yourself!"

Sheila's hand was cool and dry and forceful but Monica shrank from that terrible accusing voice.

"I've been hearing such things— I've been in New York—Why didn't you ever answer the telephone, God damn you—" Sheila cried. "You're a virtual skeleton, you're burning with fever, you must be dehydrated," she said, panting, as Monica regarded her through sleep-gummed

yes, too exhausted to defend herself. Sheila's face was
dark with blood, her eyes very nearly glittered with rage,
with disgust, she leaned over Monica saying, "Why didn't
you answer your fucking telephone don't you know I've
called and *called* and now—now—now when I haven't
any time to spare—"

Monica made a feeble gesture of dismissal and Sheila
seized her thin wrist and squeezed it hard, hard. How she
would have liked to pummel Monica, how she burned to
slap that burning face, hard—!

26

MONICA WOULD PROTEST, Monica would insist that Sheila go away and leave her alone, but she is too weak; and in any case Sheila is too excited to listen.

For Sheila Trask must have her way, no matter the grief and shame to Monica.

Such theatrics, such melodrama: an ambulance speeding along the country roads, spinning red light, siren sounding intermittently, Monica bundled in white and strapped securely in place, tears scalding her cheeks. She is going to die, she is not going to die, not if Sheila Trask has her way, and Sheila Trask *must* have her way.

Once in the ambulance, once moving along, Sheila grows calmer; her panting breath subsides; she would fumble into her pocket for cigarettes except (of course) smoking is forbidden. She is swearing under her breath, seated close beside Monica, rocking slightly from side to side in the very rage of her predicament. "You shouldn't have done this— you shouldn't have doubted me—we'll be friends for a long, long time," she says, "—unless one of us dies."

Bestselling Books
from Berkley

___ $4.50 09291-7 **THE ACCIDENTAL TOURIST**
Anne Tyler

___ $4.50 09103-1 **ELVIS AND ME**
Priscilla Beaulieu Presley with
Sandra Harmon

___ $5.95 07704-7 **"...AND LADIES OF THE CLUB"**
Helen Hooven Santmyer

___ $4.50 08520-1 **THE AUERBACH WILL**
Stephen Birmingham

___ $4.50 09077-9 **EVERYTHING AND MORE**
Jacqueline Briskin

___ $4.50 08973-8 **SAVANNAH** Eugenia Price

___ $4.50 09868-0 **DINNER AT THE HOMESICK
RESTAURANT** Anne Tyler

___ $4.50 08472-8 **LOVE, HONOR AND BETRAY**
Elizabeth Kary

___ $4.50 08529-5 **ILLUSIONS OF LOVE** Cynthia Freeman

___ $3.95 08659-3 **MATTERS OF THE HEART**
Charlotte Vale Allen

___ $3.95 08783-2 **TOO MUCH TOO SOON**
Jacqueline Briskin

___ $3.95 09204-6 **SOLSTICE** Joyce Carol Oates

___ $4.50 09203-8 **TO SEE YOUR FACE AGAIN**
Eugenia Price

___ $8.95 09670-X **PRAIRIE**
Anna Lee Waldo (Trade edition)

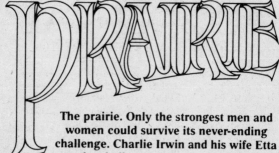